AMPLY REWARDED

DESTINY MOON

Amply Rewarded
ISBN # 978-1-78184-592-9
©Copyright Destiny Moon 2012
Cover Art by Oliver Bennett ©Copyright October 2012
Interior text design by Claire Siemaszkiewicz
Total-E-Bound Publishing

Published in 2013 by Total-E-Bound Publishing, Think Tank, Ruston Way, Lincoln, LN6 7FL, United Kingdom.

AMPLY REWARDED

Chapter One

Glendale

I grew up in Glendale, Idaho, miles from anywhere that mattered and whole states away from the cities I dreamed of. Other kids grew up collecting the usual objects — stuffed animals, stamps, stickers. I didn't care for any of that. I collected money. Once I had enough of it, I reckoned, I would have a ticket out and that mattered more to me than any toy ever could. Until then, I would placate myself with soap operas.

Houses on farms are measured differently than houses in the city. Ours, it seemed, was majestic. Even though I'd never been to any big cities, or any cities outside Idaho, I knew that everything was different there. There was no shortage of people who confirmed that fact — it's just that they always assumed they were preaching to the converted. "Glendale is a great place to raise a family," they'd say.

My sister, Faith, and I did not have many playmates. Glendale is an isolated farming village, and no one ever came to visit. We were miles off the main road that was miles off the main interstate highway. Our social life consisted of the church and each other.

But, at home, we had it all. There was a beautiful pond, over which my father had constructed a swing that was ours alone. Our mother was a fantastic baker and, since we lived in the midst of the finest orchards, she made decadent pies and tarts all summer long. Her happiness came from serving my father and us. I didn't have the heart to deprive her of that desire so I never offered to help. My sister, who loved to seem more selfless than me, would rush into the kitchen in the morning and find out what was on the agenda. If it was blueberry pie, she would grab the basket that my mother usually used, throw on a smock and scurry down to the bushes to pick the berries. Her seeming servitude disgusted me. I knew that she did what she did so that my mother would call her a good little girl and ask her to sit on the kitchen counter while she rolled the pie shells. They would both cast knowing glances my way when the time came to eat pie, as though all along they had wanted my help and I had withheld it. I never deprived anyone of anything that they didn't willingly give up.

But, in those days of summer, I had better things to do. Most of my day I spent on the swing my father had built, which my sister complained I greedily hoarded. At any time she could have claimed it as her own, but she never did. She preferred life in the kitchen, on my mother's tail, to fending for herself outside with me.

The time alone served me well. Every summer, I made it my goal to collect as much money as I could into my hidden tin. Mostly, this meant keeping the little gifts given to me by the produce dealers who drove out to our farm to buy our famous fruits and vegetables. We had a stand out front that my father's apprentices usually tended, but that I sometimes took care of. When I was there, the older men that pulled up would slow down before stopping and peer out of the window at me in my white summer dress. They always found something to give me and tried to win my favour with gifts.

My sister and the other girls from church were afraid of men, but I never understood their fear. I suppose it was my boldness that paid off in the end. It wasn't their offering but my boldness to ask that filled my tin every summer with more and more money that I kept hidden from everyone.

Sometimes they would pay me just a tiny bit more than the total they owed, and would flash me a smile and tell me that they enjoyed my service more than my father's or that of his hired help. I'd smile and nod and, when the truck pulled away on the old dirt road, I'd put the little token in my pocket and think about how much more my tin contained. It was amazing what men would do to make a little girl smile.

There are several types of men, and I learned to identify them and use their weaknesses against them. Some men responded to outright professionalism, like my father's friend Frank. He had raised five boys, all long gone now, and with his wife gone too, he came out to our farm for my mom's baking. I was straightforward with him. I'd walk right up to him and say, "Hello, Frank. Can I have a dollar?" The first time, it caught him off guard.

"What if I don't have a dollar?" He patted the top of my head.

"Hmm, well, I know you have a bill clip in your pocket, because you leave a few dollars on my mom's windowsill for the pies every week. So I know they're in there and I'm just asking if I can have one." I was reasonable and forthright.

"And what if I ask you what you're going to spend it on?"

"I'd say I'm saving it."

"For what?"

"For my future."

He laughed. "Oh, well, aren't you clever?" he said, and patted my head once more. Then he handed over a faded—yet perfectly fine—dollar bill and shook my hand. He found me amusing and never denied me the dollar. Over the years it became our ritual. It was his toll fee, and I held out my hand and nodded my head with the kind of authority that I'd seen officials use on television. We both laughed, and I filled a whole tin with Frank's crumpled dollar bills.

By the time I got a little older, I became obsessed with the idea of leaving Glendale to become a rich lady, like the kind they showed on daytime television. The women that lived dangerous lives in exciting cities. The women who woke up to vanities and dozens of the finest department store perfumes.

There was no such thing in Glendale. My mom had an old bottle of perfume that smelt of lily of the valley and an even older bottle of a musky perfume with the label worn off. She'd had these for as long as I could remember and, even though she never used them, they were prominently displayed on her bedside table, like coveted jewels.

I wanted nothing to do with my parents' lives. My dad wanted to show me how to run the business. I was the daughter of choice to take over after him, and I was flattered. I didn't know how I would tell him—but I knew I would eventually have to—that I was going to move to the coast, to San Francisco or Los Angeles or New York, and I was going to make it big. Of course, I said nothing.

On Sundays, my father would haul us off to church in his pickup. My parents sat in the front of the truck's cabin, Faith and I sat in the back on the folding benches and the workers sat in the very back, outside the cabin. This order meant something to my dad. In my father's household, everyone knew their place. The man was the head of the household and everyone passively accepted that, except me.

The church itself jutted out of the landscape in the most unnatural way, with an enormous cross that stretched up to the sky, serving to remind the parishioners of how small we ordinary people are compared to the greatness of the church. The minister disgusted me. He was an old, lecherous man who spat as he preached to his tiny congregation and seemed to feel superior to all of us. His favourite subject was greed, and he would go on and on about how content we should all be with little. How humble we should be. Of course this did not stop him from asking my mother, who could never say no to a minister, to supply baked goods every Sunday to the social that followed the sermon. There were only twenty or so women in the congregation and my mother was the best baker by far. Faith was happy with the arrangement because it meant that she could spend every Saturday with my mother. If she could, my sister would still have been nursing at my mother's breast back then, when she was eleven and twelve and thirteen. And my mother, downtrodden by all her lost dreams and the life that surrounded her, was flattered by my sister's supplication.

One time, the minister attempted a private lesson on values. He cornered me at the social and asked me to describe, in great detail, the work I did for my father at the fruit stand. He was also a visitor to our orchard and enjoyed our fruit as much as anyone. He asked if I had ever sinned with the men that visited. Had I ever taken anything from them? Or offered them anything? He said he wanted to encourage my generosity of labour and time, that my father would be pleased with me if I could develop steady visitation from loyal customers. Then he put his warm, cupped hand on my shoulder and ran it down my arm. His eyes looked into me and devoured me with the same salivating appetite that he ate my mother's pies with. I thought him a pathetic specimen to have to lean on the storytelling of a nineteen-year-old ingénue for his pleasures. That was the reason I withheld my tales about Tommy, my father's apprentice.

* * * *

Tommy was way younger than my father, but wanted to be just like him. He idolised the life my dad had and swore that, since his wild days were over, he would try to get on track, save some money and buy a house. I liked hearing about the wild days.

He used to invite me to help him with the apples. Our apple trees were the farthest from the farmhouse. Together, we walked through tall grasses down the groves and around the bend of my father's land. Once out of everyone's sight, Tommy showed me sides of himself that nobody else saw. It was in the orchard that he gave me my first education on pleasuring men.

Tommy chased me, grabbed onto my waist and I ran, laughing—we were playful like that. I had always been a good runner and therefore had never been caught, but there was something about Tommy—his brute strength, his dark skin—that made me want to be caught, if only to see what the next part of the game involved.

We tumbled to the ground. He tickled me and I laughed and laughed. We rolled around together like tumbleweed until I ended up sitting on him, my legs wrapped around his waist, his sweaty arms wrapped around me. The sun beat down on us through the slight shelter of the apple trees and we kissed. It was so gentle...in the beginning. Within days, my lips touched so many more parts of him than his lips.

He explored my body with amazement. His eyes were shocked and delighted each time I revealed a little more of myself and felt the warmth of the summer sun on my bare skin. It was as though he were doing this for the first time. I knew that could not be true, because I spent many nights hiding on ceiling planks in the barn, listening to the men talk about women they had known and what had happened. Tommy had the most to tell, but always went last. In retrospect, he was just as virginal as I was but, back in those orchard days, I would have insisted he knew all there was to know about pleasing women.

Tommy taught me to enjoy my body. His strong hands felt raspy and rough against my skin as he reached underneath my dress, up past my stomach, along my side to my breasts. His thick fingers circled my nipples and I could feel myself wanting more and more of the sensation he was giving me. My body writhed with delight, and I moved from where I had been sitting, on the lawn, to my favourite position — straddling him on his lap. My nipples stuck out, and were so much harder than I could make them myself, when I touched them in private.

I wanted more. I became a slave to the insatiable desires of my nipples, as though they functioned independently of me.

One day, we were secluded out in the orchard. I couldn't stand the pulsing sensation between my legs any longer. To Tommy's amazement—he had always called me a lady—I tore off my dress and panties and sat down on him, completely naked. I arched myself back so that my nipples were at the level of his mouth. He sucked with passion and disbelief.

I was excited at once by my body and by the idea that this should not be happening, that my father had sternly warned me against associating with men. What was I to do? There was nothing I wanted more than Tommy's tongue on my breasts. Until, of course, I wanted Tommy's tongue all over.

I felt the swelling underneath his work pants. He wanted to share it with me, as if it were a precious gift. I took his enthusiasm as an offering of knowledge. I welcomed it by unzipping him and loosening the constraint on his cock. He was already hard and his discomfort showed. His face expressed relief when his cock was finally free. It was stunning. Intuitively, and with the same greediness that he'd shown when he'd sucked on my nipples, I took him into my mouth.

It was delicious, like the first ripe fruit of the season. I guiltily gorged and tried to hide more and more of it in my mouth. He collaborated by taking my head between his hands and moving me up and down his shaft as he emitted loud, encouraging moans. Time seemed to stand still as we moved together in bliss. Just when I became accustomed to our rhythm, I felt an urgency build in him. It made me quiver with lust and curiosity. He used strong hands to move my head faster and faster until he almost yelped and released a gigantic pool of juice into my mouth.

He lifted my head and studied my facial expression with an intensity that I had never been given. His offering slid down my throat and I licked my lips. Then he kissed me.

* * * *

I became addicted to our shared interest. I learned how to take him from calm and flaccid to abundant and giving with my mouth, my hands and my breasts. To my knowledge, he didn't talk about it with the other men, perhaps for fear of what my father would do. I was pleased that he had not jeopardised our secret. I had not learned everything I could from him. I wanted him to take my virginity but he told me to be less eager. That was not our only difference of opinion.

Tommy was not only a gentleman but — poor thing — he was also a man in love. Somehow, in his mind, he had equated my acceptance of his tutelage with my acceptance of him. He wanted us to slow down, he said. He wanted us to be more tender with each other. He asked me to go with him to Boise on a shopping trip.

"To the farm equipment supplier? How exciting." By then, I had mastered the miracle of sarcasm.

Tommy was about five years older than me and had long since passed his sarcastic phase, if he had ever had one. He was seldom as amused by me as I was. "Come with me, Julie. I want us to look at something. Something nice."

As soon as the words came out of his mouth, I was panic-stricken. I didn't know what exactly he was referring to, but I could tell that I wouldn't approve. I'm not exactly sure why, but I went along with it. Inexperience meant I didn't have gracious ways of getting out of undesirable situations.

Three hours later, we were in Boise. Tommy pulled into a strip mall that had a jewellery store, a pet store and a grocery store. My pulse raced through my body.

"Julie, I've been thinking…" He wasn't looking me in the eye anymore, but staring straight ahead at the noisy traffic. "You really mean a lot to me and I want to get you something special."

Focusing on the pet store, I said, "I don't know, Tommy. I mean, kittens and puppies are a big commitment and I'm just not sure I'm ready."

"Julie, c'mon, be serious. I'm talking about a ring here."

"What for? You going to ask me to marry you, or something?"

"Well, maybe not just yet…"

"I should think not, Tommy. I'm only nineteen."

"But in a couple of years…"

It was worse than I had anticipated. Because I had been afraid of this inevitable talk, I had imagined it many times in my head. In my imagination—unlike now—I'd always come across as thoughtful and diplomatic.

"Tommy, that's really sweet but you're my first…well…boyfriend… If that's what you are… I mean… C'mon… You work for my father…and… Well… I'm young…"

"That's why I said in a couple of years. I want to get you a promise ring. And then, when the time is right—"

"When the time is right?" I interrupted him because I hated the ease with which the words rolled off his tongue. "Then what, Tommy? You'll propose? Then what? We'll get married, move into a house—or, worse, stay at the farm... Move into my parents' bedroom? Is that what you want?" The idea was vile. Years of a possible future flashed before my eyes and repulsed me.

"I love you, Julie."

He played it as if it were a magic hand he had been dealt at cards.

"Oh, bullshit," I said.

"What?"

"You heard me. You don't love me. You just love the idea of me. Keep working at the farm, take over the family business, the family daughter."

"You're awful. How can you even say that? And how dare you tell me how I feel?"

"Get out."

"What?"

"You heard me. Get out."

He was as mad as anyone would be who was three hours away from home and knew they were about to be dropped off and left behind. I didn't have a choice. I suppose I could have been nicer about the whole thing, but that would just have encouraged him. It would have given him a sliver of hope that we shared a mutual vision for our lives, which we did not.

As I shoved over to the driver's side, fastened my seatbelt and reversed out of the parking stall, I took a look at Tommy in my rear-view mirror. He was cursing and kicking the pavement and flailing his arms about. I felt sorry for him at the same time as I felt I had narrowly escaped a horrid future with this grubby, small-minded man. A promise ring? What was he thinking? We had barely fooled around, and already he wanted to shack up with me? Linda Evans would have said no, too.

* * * *

When I pulled up to the plot of lawn where we keep the truck, my mom came running out of the house. "Show me the ring," she cooed, rubbing her floured hands on her apron. She stopped short of hugging me. "Where's Tommy?"

"You knew about this?"

"Well...uh... Your father told me not to say anything, but they had a little chat the other night and..."

It was the worst conspiracy I'd ever had the displeasure of witnessing. I knew I'd have to leave this place. My parents were all too set on the idea of my furthering their ambitions. I couldn't bear the thought of not seeing the world, of not knowing what it felt like to make it on my own. If Tommy wanted to stay here, let him. As for the farm, it was a clear oversight on my parents' part to only have the two of us, and unfortunate that my sister was so useless.

* * * *

"What'd you do with Tommy?" my father asked, by way of opening up the dinner conversation.

"I dropped him off in Boise."

"In Boise?"

"Yep."

"What, the ring he gave you wasn't big enough or something?"

"Not big enough at all."

Faith gave me a dirty look and my parents just looked as if I'd committed the worst sin imaginable. After a lot of uncomfortable throat clearing, my mom picked up where Dad had left off.

"I can't believe your biggest objection is the size of the ring."

"If you knew me at all, you'd know I wasn't talking about the ring. My dreams are bigger than all of this."

I pushed my chair out, marched past her, out into the orchard, and kept on walking. I didn't want to talk to anyone for a while. I had been taken aback by the tone of my own voice. The strength of my words came from my heart and they were true, but as soon as I'd said them I'd known I'd said something they would not understand. They'd never be able to comprehend my thoughts, ambitions, feelings or beliefs. We were so different.

When I came back into the house, everyone was still in the kitchen eating. A hush came over the room when I walked in and sat down. I filled my plate and, just as I began to eat my lumpy mashed potatoes, I saw my father's smirk. The only sound in the room was cutlery on plates. Everyone averted their eyes.

"Why, I just can't believe you can make a fella walk all the way from Boise. That's a good day of walking," my father said. Everyone at the table laughed.

"You owe me my best guy," he continued. "Maybe Tommy's not your dream man, but he is mine. So I'll expect you bright and early out there since you seen to it that my guy's nowhere around."

I couldn't argue with my father. His verdict was fair and I set my alarm, got up at five and joined him and the other men outside in my work clothes. The harvest stops for no one.

I was sitting on a barrel, eating an apple, when I spied Tommy's figure at the gate. A couple of the guys ran over to him and my father, somewhat instinctively, turned to him. I took it all as my cue to go inside for a while. I liked watching soap operas but being in one was not my style.

I'd thought we had been discreet. I'd thought no one had known. Finding out that they had was not only devastating, but it irked me. I'd always had my secret plan, my secret version of myself, and the way they all looked at me now, I could tell the only version of me they saw was Tommy's.

* * * *

However secret we'd kept ourselves before, news spread about the cruel way I'd rejected Tommy. Everyone disapproved of me and offered their sympathies to him. It was so typical. Faith told me I'd made the worst choice of my life and that now I'd never find a decent man, since I'd ruined things with Tommy. She could be so dramatic.

"He's like every other man," I told Faith. "I could get him back like that if I wanted." I snapped my fingers.

"You could not."

"Watch me."

The dare was on. I had never lost an argument with Faith about anything. With my naïve sister in tow, I went to our room, where I changed into my white summer dress. Of all my clothes, this dress was the most revealing of my cleavage. I peeled off my panties and tossed them under my covers. Faith followed me out back to where the men were working.

"Tommy? Can I have a moment with you?"

He cocked his head to one side, confused by my friendly tone. "Sure."

I took him by the hand and led him off to the orchard. I turned back and gestured to Faith to follow us, which she did not. I felt like I'd won already.

On the way to the orchard, Tommy said, "I'm heartbroken."

"Don't be so sentimental," I said.

"I wanted to you to be my wife and you just laughed at me. Do you have any idea what that does to a guy?"

"It wasn't personal. It's not you I find laughable — it's marriage."

"Marriage?"

"The whole charade of it, the idea of one woman and one man acknowledging before God and man that they will only ever love each other."

"What's wrong with that?"

"Nothing, but it's not the way my heart works. And the idea that marriage means monogamy. I find that laughable, too."

"You do?" He was incredulous.

"Of course. I've heard you talk about other women. I know you have needs."

"Oh, Julie. You overheard us? Oh, baby, I'm sorry. That wasn't for your ears. That's just how guys talk. I was making it up."

"It's okay, Tommy. It's natural. I have needs, too."

"I was planning on taking good care of your needs once we got married."

"I know, Tommy. Let's just skip the marriage part and I'll let you take care of my needs right now."

"Julie, it's wrong."

"No, it isn't."

I ran my hand down his front, feeling for his bulge. Even though I didn't want to spend the rest of my life with him, I sure did appreciate the hulking gorgeousness that was Tommy. I felt him harden inside his jeans.

"Julie, I'm confused."

"Don't think so much, Tommy. Just let me take care of you."

I unzipped his jeans and reached in to pull out his semi-erect penis. Holding it in my hand made me feel powerful. I stroked him.

"I don't know if this is a good idea."

"Trust me, it is."

"But, Julie..."

"Shhh."

I squatted down in front of him and took him in my mouth. I had big plans for him and the very thought that today was the day got me so wet I could feel myself throbbing. My summer dress rested on my thighs and I spread my legs apart and touched myself. I was soaked. I ran my forefinger and middle finger over my moisture. Then I paused my attention on Tommy's cock so that I could stand up and shove my juicy fingers into his mouth.

"Oh, Julie," he moaned after tasting me. "You aren't wearing underwear. You are relentless."

"That I am," I said. "So you better surrender."

He nodded. I pulled his jeans off, and he took his shirt off and placed it on the ground. I got him to sit on his shirt, then climbed on top of him, like I had before, but this time I slowly placed his hard cock at my wet opening.

He shook his head in disbelief. "I can't believe this," he said.

I eased him into me and felt my muscles squeeze and tighten around him. I'd always heard that the first time was supposed to be painful, but mine wasn't. His cock felt so good inside me. I moaned and gasped at the pleasure of it all, the feeling of being filled up, of my pussy stretching to accommodate his impressive girth. I lowered myself completely onto him. He was so deep inside me that I felt like I couldn't take any more. Then I pushed his chest back so that he was lying down and began riding him. The feeling was so natural, so utterly easy for me. Inside, I felt him stiffen even more. This was unlike anything I'd experienced before and everything about it pleased me, especially the knowledge that this was a dare to prove myself right to Faith. I wondered if she was hiding somewhere in the bushes watching, but I was quite sure I'd already satisfactorily made my point and she'd gone home, horrified by her sister's immorality.

I rode Tommy so hard that I pounded the earth beneath us each time I lowered myself onto him. I'm sure we made the apple trees shake above us. I felt a tingling build within me, an energy that grew from somewhere deep inside my being. I wanted release. I needed it. Leaning forward just slightly, I felt the rub of his skin against my clitoris. He cupped my breasts in his hands. I cupped his hands in mine and guided his fingers to squeeze my nipples, which he did obediently.

"Mmm," I moaned. "A little harder and I'm going to come."

"Oh, my God," he gasped. His mind could not keep up with our animal behaviour. His disbelief only encouraged my orgasm. There was so much pleasure in blowing his mind.

"Yeah, that's it. Can you feel me?"

He nodded.

His commitment to satisfying my needs was delightful. I squeezed his cock with my vaginal muscles, feeling every nuance of our bodies against each other. And just as I was finding the rhythm of our friction again, something took over inside me. It was as though my clitoris and nipples were steering me, directing all of my movements to intensify the build-up of energy. Then there was the total surrender to pleasure. Everything around us disappeared. If Faith or anyone had been watching, I wouldn't have seen. If it had started to rain, I wouldn't have noticed. I wouldn't have felt an earthquake. All my senses heightened to a level I'd never experienced before and my breath quickened. I could feel my heart pounding. My pulse raced through me and I felt as though I were encased in a blanket of soft silk. Everything surrendered to the feeling of bliss that overcame me.

Tommy took me in his firm embrace and held me tight as my pussy spasmed around his shaft. He clutched me to him and I collapsed onto him, savouring his embrace. Sharing my orgasm with him was like nothing I'd ever experienced.

"Julie, you are so beautiful," he said.

I rested my head on his chest and recovered from the sheer exhaustion my body felt. He caressed my back and held me tight, his cock still hard inside me, though motionless. He took my hips in his strong hands and held me in place while he thrust his cock into me again. I was so sensitive that his movement made me squirm.

"Can I come?" he asked.

"Do you want to come in my pussy?"

He nodded. I moaned at the thought of it. My clitoris hardened at the idea. I'd been preparing for this very moment by taking the pill regularly since I'd started fooling around with him.

"Oh? How badly?" I teased.

"I'll do anything for you." He sounded so earnest.

"That's what I like to hear," I said, and lifted my torso just slightly, tightening my vaginal grip as I gyrated on him.

"Oh, Julie. Oh, Julie. Oh, Julie. I can't take it much longer." His voice sounded as if he were in pain — sweet, delicious pain. His cock was so hard inside me.

"Then fill me up," I whispered into his ear. With that he emitted a loud moan and grabbed me by my hips, pulling me so tightly onto him that I felt every movement of his throbbing cock as he released. It was so warm, so satisfying. We stayed like that for a long while. His cock receded very slowly, finally slipping out of me in what felt like the ultimate relaxation. He wanted to kiss me but I didn't let him, preferring to rest on his chest, in his arms. It felt so good and right.

"So I guess we're back together again," he observed. Poor Tommy.

"Let's not be hasty," I said.

He sat up, alarmed. His body language betrayed him. He went from completely calm to highly agitated. "I don't understand you," he said, and looked away.

"I told you already. It's not personal. I just don't want any of the same stuff you do. But I'm glad we shared this. I've wanted it for a long time and it was perfect."

"Perfect? Hardly. Julie, I just took your virginity. Does that mean nothing to you?"

"It means a lot to me," I said, trying to sway his mood. He was so much more enjoyable in his relaxed state. "Anyway, you didn't take anything. I gave it to you."

"Well, you took mine." He put on his shirt and buttoned it up.

"Excuse me?"

"You heard me," he said indignantly.

"But... All those stories in the barn."

"I told you. That was just man talk." He stood up and pulled his jeans on, zipped them up and sat down beside me again, looking forlorn.

"You mean fiction?"

"Well... Yeah, I guess."

This was unfathomable. "Tommy, you can't put that on me."

"I'm not putting anything on you, Julie," he said emphatically, imitating me in a rather unflattering way. "I'm in love with you. That's why I made love to you. Isn't that why you made love to me?"

This was beginning to feel quite manipulative. I hadn't thought he had that kind of complexity in him. His eyes were so hopeful, so innocent, as though he wanted me to jump into his narrative and behave exactly like his fantasy version of me. Instead, I shook my head.

"No, Tommy. I'm not in love with you."

He sighed. "I just don't understand you, Julie. I suppose I never will."

Silently, I stood up. We walked solemnly back through the orchard. I felt his semen trickle down my inner thigh. It felt cool as the breeze hit it.

* * * *

That spring, a man in a suit visited my father several times. They took walks together around the garden so that their conversations could not be overheard. My mother sobbed many times in the kitchen. I walked in on her cuddling up to the antique buffet, clenching her apron in her fist and hiding her head inside her bent arm, crying.

My father finally made the announcement that we were bankrupt and had to flee. My mother, who had no intention of ever leaving, refused to listen to his logic that we take a train and start a new life somewhere else. She importuned him with the tiniest details, demanding to know who would replace her in baking for the congregation, and what would happen to her beautiful hydrangeas. My father fought with my mother for days. Afterward, he announced his departure to my sister and me, and he packed his suitcase and calmly walked out of the front door, down the pathway to his truck. He got in and drove away. I never saw him after that. He made no effort to contact us and we had no clue where he went.

My mother became ill immediately after my father left. My sister tried uselessly to help her, but she needed my mother's strength to validate her efforts and my mother could not offer it. She was in bed for a week, then she died. All my life I'd endured her judgements, her strict rules and hypocrisy. For better or worse, everything disappeared along with her. My sister was devastated. She cried for days. I knew I would cry eventually, but I had a far more pressing concern – survival.

I tried to convince Faith that staying would be futile. The authorities were already making weekly visits to our property to collect the taxes my father owed. What would they do when they saw that we were living there alone now? We could not possibly run a profitable farm, they would say. Then they would take her and throw her into an orphanage or a convent or some horrid place. I told my sister that she should never let it happen to her. She had never foreseen the possibility of being alone in the world and had no idea how to handle it. I'd always known that my dreams were big and that I alone was responsible for making them happen.

It irritated me that my sister didn't understand her value, even when I told her what it was. I was candid. I told her the truth—that she was beautiful. She had long, blonde hair that cascaded about her shoulders. Her eyes were doe-like and clear blue, and, if she hadn't been my sister, I know I could have lost myself in those eyes, which were so responsive that she could express every emotion without ever opening her mouth. I told her how many of the weekend visitors would ask about her as they hauled away their boxes of produce. It was a blessing to be desired, but she didn't see it that way.

This information disgusted her. I tried to convince her it was a good thing. I told her that neither one of us ever had to worry about starvation. I told her about the woman in the congregation who was half the age of her rather repugnant husband. I told her what I had overheard some years ago. She had been alone and desolate when she'd met him, and she'd pretended she'd been travelling and had been robbed of her passport, money and luggage. He'd stopped for her on the old dirt road where she was walking and had taken her in for the night. Now they were married and, even though she did not seem particularly happy, she was obviously well fed.

I pointed out that we knew many men just in and around our property, and if we were willing to go into the world, we would undoubtedly find more. Men were the easiest key to survival, but Faith didn't understand.

My story did nothing positive for my sister. She was daunted by my suggestion. She told me I was wretched, sordid and filthy and that she didn't want to have anything to do with someone who would even consider using her God-given beauty in such a lewd way.

"Suit yourself," I said. I vowed never to feel sympathy for her in all of her self-righteousness.

"I'm marrying Tommy," she announced. Her tone implied that she meant for this information to sting. It didn't. I would have taken care of her out of the sense of responsibility that older, smarter siblings inherently have towards their inferior younger ones, but I was relieved that I wouldn't have to.

"Congratulations."

I went upstairs and packed my clothes. I took my mother's wedding ring in my palm and studied it. It had meant so much to her. I didn't understand it. There was a sombre emptiness in my stomach, but also a sense of adventure and freedom greater than any I'd ever known. I said a prayer for my mom. I left the ring on Faith's pillow. Taking one last glance at the house that had been my home for all of my twenty years would have been a mistake, and I still have no regretful sentiment that I did not keep a picture of that day in my mind.

I was twenty by the time I left. I would have gone earlier if I'd had the money. After five years of saving my meagre weekend earnings, hidden, I had accumulated enough to buy a ticket to the coast and to stay in a hotel for two or three nights. It had been my plan to do that, then to meet a rich gentleman—like the ones that pulled in at the weekends to buy produce, only richer and urbane. I wanted to leave and not come back until I had made something of myself.

It wasn't long before my feet grew tired from walking. I had been on the dirt road for hours and dusk had set in. It was time to placate myself with reminders of how I would succeed and how this summer would be the turning point I needed in order to grow. I had everything I could possibly need to survive—right there with me as I walked.

It was the loneliest I'd ever felt, and the most reverent. Emotions always present themselves best with their antithesis. This was the culmination of every feeling I'd had in years. I was despondent as well as determined. I had to look forward.

Chapter Two

The Road

I spent the first night in an abandoned barn, using my other dress as my blanket and the hay inside the almost crumbling building as my insulation. The air was warm. Sounds of mosquitoes kept me awake for quite a long time after dark. Then my fears set in. I was so tremulous that I could not move, so I closed my eyes and slept. I was glad that I could experience this kind of fear alone and live through it. My rational sensibility that I was safer in that abandoned barn than any other place I could have ended up that night kept my vision focused and I assured myself that I didn't need to rely on anyone else — I had a great relationship with myself and I would nurture and take care of myself from then on, and do it proudly.

Idaho had served me well. But it was all I knew. A couple of years ago, my dad had hooked up a salvaged satellite dish that, to our collective surprise, had worked. So, without knowing anything about California but what I had seen on TV, I had made up my mind that San Francisco would be my city. It would be the place where things would happen for me because they had happened for so many other people.

I made my way to the nearest town in the county, Old Cliffe, by hitchhiking. I had been there many times. It was a good junction to go to because it had a bus depot and I could catch a Greyhound there. Of course, I soon realised I'd have more money to spend once I got to San Francisco if I afforded myself the company of strangers.

Hitching was effortless. Men stopped for me and each of the rides out to the coast gave me more insight into the male psyche. They wanted to know me in exchange for the ride they were giving me, and they all learned that I didn't work like that.

I was such a temptress then. I could get a man to drive me in the opposite direction to the one he had been headed merely by batting my eyelashes and crossing my legs in his direction. Men are simple creatures and I had learned basic manipulation tactics long ago. During the trip, which took the better part of a week, I practiced my skills. I read faces, gestures and rhetoric. I could tell who was Christian, who was a father and who was a scared pervert too nervous to take advantage of me. And I worked on the conscience of each of them. Most of them gave me money when I told them I had run away from my abusive home life in search of a grandmother I'd only heard of and never met. And I made sure to tell each of them how vital they were to my success and I convinced them that helping me was the one thing they wanted more than anything else. I slept in a hotel room every night on somebody else's dime. I was surprised and delighted with myself for making the journey work that way. Had I been sceptical of my ability to seduce people into doing nice things for me, that trip would have assured me I was exactly the seductress I'd convinced myself I could be. But then it was all still so new.

Growing up with farmhands around me, I'd learned to eavesdrop on conversations for information about the real world outside Glendale. I knew that big cities offered advantages to girls like me, and that all I had to do was find the right woman to teach me and take me under her wing.

* * * *

San Francisco

I asked one of my drivers to pull over and wait while I went to the ladies' room and, as usual, my command was obeyed. Inside by the pay phone, I saw a stand with newspapers. I looked for the alternative free distribution kind and leafed through the back pages. *High rates for beautiful young girls, minimal nudity, full discretion, please call.* Between the ads for massage parlours were ads that girls had posted themselves. Even if my biggest dreams didn't pan out right away, I wouldn't starve. I left through the back door without thanking the ride that had taken me the final seventy miles of my journey. I had made it to San Francisco. I had plenty of money tucked in my backpack and a mind full of dreams.

I kept the newspaper with all the ads, for future reference. It was early afternoon and I was embarking on the most exciting part of my journey.

Walking through the streets felt like magic. There was something about the momentum of the city that exuded hope and newness. The boredom of my past was over. This was the beginning of everything.

I'd spent the past week trying on various personas for my drivers and I needed to recuperate. Enough lying. I was here to find myself and make it big. I thought I would start by walking up and down the busy streets, stepping in and out of coffee houses as I pleased. I would be whimsical about my accommodations, find the part of town that suited me and settle in.

I started to feel as though I was in the wrong neighbourhood when men ogled me with their overly familiar stares. The looks in their eyes were anything but respectful. *You wait*, I told them in my head, *you just wait*. I could play along for now — I was a nobody, a complete stranger to this world — but it would not take long for me to become the kind of woman who commanded a whole different kind of attention. I turned on my heels and headed for the financial district.

It was around dinnertime when I settled into the Side Bar, the first place with a name I recognised from the back pages of the newspaper. I followed a bunch of executives in suits who were talking about the day's earnings and how they were going to grab some drinks and hang out with the Friday night girls. Inside, the place was a little grim. It was like what I had seen in old black and white movies — a smoke-filled room with stern-looking waitresses, male patrons and jazz.

The hostess who greeted me seemed confused. I guessed this wasn't the type of place women came to alone, so I played along.

"I'm meeting someone. Could I get a table for two?"

"Oh, sure." She looked me up and down, searched for a couple of laminated menus and told me to follow her. "You wanna be able to see the dancers or not?"

"Yes, please."

I was seated around the corner from the bar, at a small round table. I ordered a martini because I'd never had one and I needed to rectify that. When the bartender asked for my ID, I told him I was twenty-five and, shockingly, he believed me. I also got potato skins, my one homage to my past life.

I couldn't take my eyes off the girls on the stage. There were two of them doing a wild set of moves. They seemed so free. I couldn't imagine what it must feel like to have so many people's attention at the same time. They seemed to enjoy it until their kissing scene, when I saw one of their faces and she looked drab, completely emotionless, like a machine. I wondered if she had been doing it for too long, or if she had just never enjoyed it. Maybe she wanted to be kissing her friend, just not in public like that. Whatever the reason, her eyes haunted me. She seemed distant and uncommitted. But everything I questioned only made me question myself. How would *I* like it? How would *I* feel? And, especially, what good did it do to sit in an audience and speculate? This was not where answers could be found.

The other woman on the stage had the gift. She was sultry and gorgeous with expressive eyes and a body she worked like a ballerina. She was totally in control. Her confidence was intoxicating.

Not long after the number, the gifted girl came out. She was stunning, dressed in a tight, black dress with long, black, shiny boots. Her long, dark hair was complemented by her amazing dark lips. She seemed to be every man's fantasy and they all turned to watch her as she walked up to the bar. There was just something about her, something magical and enticing.

What did I know? I questioned myself. I didn't even know her. I didn't know anything about this kind of place. I had come out to the big city looking for adventure, and what could I possibly know about her life? Overwhelmed by the place, I was almost sure I didn't want what she had. I was convinced that there was something about it that she didn't like, either.

Several men approached her at the bar and seemed all too eager to buy her drinks. She graciously accepted a glass of red wine, which made her look even more seductive. She sat down at the bar, ignoring the man who had paid for her wine, and watched the rest of the show. The same girl she had kissed on stage came out again in a different costume, this time alone, and started strutting back and forth across the stage. She swung herself around the pole and my brunette started laughing and cheering and lit up the room with her enthusiasm.

Part of me didn't expect her to be nice to me. I wondered why I had such preconceived ideas about her, and whether they would be proved right. I approached her and she smiled at me. We said our awkward hellos while watching the stage and taking careful sips from our drinks. I must have looked interested because she told me the place was hiring.

"I am looking for work," I said, "but I'm not sure if this is it."

"Usually when a hot girl comes up to me it's because she wants me to introduce her to the manager. My mistake."

Well, she hadn't exactly made a mistake, and I couldn't help but feel flattered that she'd basically stated that I was a hot girl.

"No problem. It looks like a good place to work."

"Yep. Tips are high. Management is all right. I should know. I've been here two years. Time to move on, though."

"You're leaving?"

"Retired as of about ten minutes ago."

"Wow."

"Not like that. Retired from dancing."

"To what?"

"Well, aren't you the curious one? I don't even know your name."

"Julie."

"Veronica." We shook hands. Our friendship was effortless.

"I was so taken by your presence on stage, I can't imagine why you'd move on. Forgive me. I'm being so forward. I usually don't drink. I just mean that you're really talented."

I was blubbering like a moron. It was so intimidating talking to such a bombshell. She just ate it up.

"You're adorable. Let's get you another martini."

The night was magical. It was as if we had been separated at birth, the way we finished each other's sentences and laughed at each other's jokes. Our connection was further emphasised when various men approached Veronica. She simply said, "I'm chatting with a friend. Another time."

When I told her it was my first night in town, she laughed hysterically that my place of choice to spend the evening had been the Side Bar.

"What were you thinking?"

"Well, I got to meet you, didn't I?" I was surprised at how forward I was being with her. I didn't know what I wanted from her, but I knew I liked her. I also knew I hadn't ever liked another girl that way.

"So where are you staying, then?" she asked.

"Not sure yet."

"What?" She was mortified. "Were you going to sleep in the streets? Stay here all night?"

"No. I don't know. I don't think I can sleep tonight. I'm so excited to be here."

"Here?"

"San Francisco. I've never been to the coast before."

"Where are you from?"

"Glendale, Idaho."

"Well, dang. I'm from Green Hill, Alabama. What do those two towns have to do with each other? Well, nothing, probably, except they both start with G and they're excellent places to leave."

We clinked glasses.

"Cheers," I mumbled. My fourth martini — or was it my sixth? — and everything was dandy. I hadn't known where I'd been going, but something told me I had arrived.

We left the Side Bar with Veronica kissing and hugging all the girls, while all the men tried to get her attention. She snubbed them all. I guessed after two years the novelty of their fascination had worn off.

"So, Julie, are you telling me you haven't even seen the ocean yet?"

"I haven't."

"Taxi!" She stuck her hand out in the air and put her other arm around me. I felt warm and secure and beside myself with glee. A yellow cab pulled up instantly and Veronica told the driver where to go. Twenty minutes later, we were at a gorgeous lookout point with tons of other cars parked and playing music. She whisked me out of the cab, took my hand and spun me around. Some guys in a Chevy truck up the way saw us, rolled down their window and turned up the radio.

The ocean air was salty and felt clean. I looked out at the Pacific and felt awe in a way I'd never expected. The sounds of the waves beckoned. I wanted to jump in but we were way too high up for that. We were somewhere near Golden Gate Bridge, but I couldn't see the landmark and it didn't matter. This was heaven on Earth.

"You want to stay here or go back to my place?"

"No brainer. Your place." I was too drunk to try to fend for myself now and besides, I would do anything to stay with Veronica.

"Okay, but first we have to have a dance." She grabbed my hand and we danced together. The sounds of the guys in the truck totally disappeared into background din. All I saw was Veronica and the endless vast ocean in front of me. I felt more beautiful and more alive than ever.

Chapter Three

Carla's House

The next morning, I woke up on a foldout couch in a beautiful, character-filled house and the sun was shining in on my aching head. I looked around but found no one. I wasn't scared at all, just curious. Veronica emerged from the bedroom in an oversized T-shirt, with bed-head and her dark eye makeup streaking down her cheeks.

"Hey," she said as she walked past me on her way to the bathroom. I heard the water running in her shower and I just sat on the couch with the blanket tucked around me. I wondered if she was going to ask me to leave, or what. When she came out again, her alabaster skin was clean and she had her hair tucked up in a towel. She walked by me completely naked, as though it was the most natural thing in the world. No one did that where I was from. My God, she was beautiful.

"Here. Make coffee." She handed me some filters and a jar. I boiled water, tried to figure out her system. "So, what are we going to do with you?"

"What do you mean?"

"Home. Job. You know. Where do you want to be?"

She was so upfront. She was so candid and open. She was still naked in front of me and I had been cowering, afraid to even tiptoe to the bathroom. There was definitely something about her, because my other companions over the last week hadn't seen this side of me. I hadn't even known I *had* this side. Veronica had had me spellbound from the first moment I'd seen her. I hadn't believed it possible to be so instantly infatuated with anyone.

"Well, you're free to stay here," she offered. "But I have to check with Carla."

My heart skipped a beat. "Carla?"

"She sort of runs the house. She's good. Good judge of character, if you know what I mean."

"Is she your landlord?"

Veronica laughed. I poured coffee for us and wondered what was so funny.

"Remember how you wanted to know what I was going to do after retiring from dancing? Well, you're looking at it."

I was puzzled.

"I... You know..."

I pieced it together. "Oh, my God, Veronica. Are you an escort?"

"Are you disappointed?" she asked. I thought it was a strange question.

"Not at all. I think it's great."

"I don't know if I'd go that far, but I've known Carla for a long time and this is a different kind of place than most. I have a lot more control and I can't argue with the money."

"It sounds really good."

"Are you looking for work or something?"

"Actually, I am."

"You sure this is the kind of work you want?"

I nodded. "Definitely."

"I could talk to her for you…or introduce you."

"Would you?" This was fate. But her face changed. She looked sullen, maybe sceptical. It was hard to tell, but I could feel it.

"Most girls don't just start here, you know. Have you done anything at all like this? Dancing? Hostessing?"

"No, but I learn quickly."

"I'm sure you do. Just remember, I'm trusting you and I'm about to do you a massive favour, and neither of those two things happens very often."

"I really appreciate your kindness and hospitality."

"Don't mention it. I had fun with you last night."

"Me too."

We sipped our coffee, then Veronica made toast.

"So what exactly does this work entail?" I finally asked.

She winked at me. "I can show you the ropes, but you're going to have to set up your boundaries with Carla. That's how it works."

"Lucrative?"

"Very."

"I'm in."

I took her empty mug of coffee and refilled it and wondered, if she shared this house with others, where they were.

"This is my suite. You'd have your own. Oh, it's civilised all right. And I'll tell you what else. This is a nice part of town, you know? A nice neighbourhood. Like, no one really knows what goes on here because we're all young and whatever. Carla has everyone convinced we're trust fund babies going to Berkeley."

"Seriously?"

"Sure. This is high end. Carla was pro for years. She really made a name for herself and then she became an entrepreneur, and now she's got a few of these set-ups around the city."

"That's so smart."

"Which part? The fact that she made buckets or that she figured out how to manage other girls instead of doing the work herself?"

"I was just thinking about the student housing cover-up."

"That is pretty damn smart," Veronica said. "Believe me, I'm studying her. I'm going to do the exact same thing once I've got my start-up capital."

She sounded so ambitious and sophisticated. I'd never in my whole life met a woman like her. We had a wonderful morning together. It felt as if I'd known her forever. I think it's funny with friendship—not a matter of time at all, but a matter of love. Veronica made me feel like the world was in bloom and I was right inside the most exquisite blossom watching it unfold.

I was to talk to Carla that afternoon. Veronica set it up before her first and only appointment of the day. She told me to be downstairs in Carla's office at three and to borrow something nice from her closet. I hadn't expected Veronica to be so kind and generous. I wasn't sure what I had expected. After last night's midnight beach dancing, my expectations had become irrelevant.

Downstairs, Carla was friendly, too. But intimidating. She wore a pink skirt and blazer suit with a white button-down shirt and a string of pearls. She was much more conservative than I had imagined, and much more elegant. Again, I felt naïve.

"So, Veronica filled you in on what this is all about?" she asked, crossing her legs and looking rather sternly at me over the rim of her glasses.

I nodded.

"Okay, 'cause I can't have you moving in and then moving out. If you go, it's gotta be like on semester break, or something."

I nodded.

"I built this business from the ground up," she said. "It's solid."

She seemed so powerful to me—easily the most powerful woman I'd ever met—and I really could not believe my tremendous luck to have landed such an excellent situation right away. Her bookshelves were lined with all the classics. Carla seemed decent and smart. Veronica had called her jaded but she looked too young to be. She was also beautiful. Not in the dark and mysterious way Veronica was, but in a girl-next-door sort of way.

"Why do you want to do this kind of work?" she asked.

I was thrown off by the question. I didn't understand why my motivations were relevant to her. "I enjoy taking advantage of men."

She looked at me for a while. It was awkward, to say the least.

"Some girls feel as though it is the men who take advantage of them, so your phrasing is interesting," she finally said. "Have you done this sort of thing before?"

"No," I said. "But you don't have to worry about me. I can handle this."

She still just sat there stiffly, shifting her gaze from my face to my body to her nails and back to me.

"We'll start you slow. Lots of clients just want companionship, massages, that kind of thing."

"Veronica said she could help me along, too," I offered.

"All right," she announced as she held out her hand to me. "I'm prepared to offer you a contract."

"Wow. Thank you."

"Fifty-fifty split. You get free rent and no bills."

"Sounds good to me."

"Rarely more than one client per twenty-four-hour period. I don't know what Veronica told you, but this is high end. Doctors, lawyers, that kind of thing—so spend some time reading and educating yourself. This is about presenting the entire package, not just looks."

I nodded again.

We shook hands before Carla had had a chance to ask me where I knew Veronica from, or for how long. We talked about some more details, then she handed me a wad of cash to update my wardrobe. An advance, she said.

The arrangement was that I was to stay with Veronica until Josie had cleared her stuff out of her suite. It was just the three of us and Carla didn't take visitors. She just liked this house more than any of her others, which was understandable, since it was stunning. I had always thought that these kinds of arrangement involved more people. I guess all I knew about it was from movies.

Back in Veronica's suite, she toasted me with a cup of Earl Grey tea.

"You made it. Congratulations."

"I kind of can't believe it."

"All the glamour and excitement?"

"Yeah."

"It'll wear off. Like, tomorrow. Trust me."

"What do you mean?"

"You do know what you're getting into, don't you?"

"Well, yeah."

"But have you done it?"

"Well, no."

"Well...then." She pulled a couple of cigarettes out of a package and passed one to me, then lit them both. "You're free to stay here and watch what I do, okay? But I don't want you being obvious about it. It'd be too hard for me to stay in character."

"In character?"

"Veronica."

I looked at her, puzzled. It must have been clear.

"Oh, shit," she said, "I didn't tell you my real name. It's Kelly. When I moved here, I didn't think it sounded sophisticated enough. Anyway, you're not supposed to work under your real name. Carla told you, I'm sure."

"She didn't say much, but I guess that makes sense."

"Well, listen. Watch and learn, cause it's pretty easy once you get the hang of it."

That night, I watched Kelly make five hundred bucks from her regular, Mr Stevens. Just like us, apparently most men didn't use their real names either, and first names were out of the question. If you walked by each other in the street, you weren't supposed to acknowledge each other. That was just part of the code.

Mr Stevens, Kelly suspected, was a married man. He had a thing for her schoolgirl uniform. He came straight from work, dressed in a suit, and sat all uptight in Carla's lounge downstairs, where he waited for Veronica to emerge from the en suite changing room. I hid behind a vintage wall divider in a dark corner. The thrill of having to be absolutely silent added to the experience.

Kelly came out wearing a tight, button-down white shirt with black pinstripe mini skirt. Her hair was in a chignon, as if she were a sexy librarian. She wore a ton of eye makeup, but Mr Stevens didn't look at her face. He was so entranced with her body and her bare midriff.

"Oh, Veronica, I've missed you."

"Why haven't you come to see me, Mr Stevens?" Kelly cooed.

"I'm here now." He patted his knee. "Come and sit with me."

She went straight for his lap and put her arms around his neck.

"Oh, that's my girl," he said, closing his eyes momentarily. "I brought you a little something."

He handed her a wrapped box. She tore off the wrapping paper and pulled out a pair of panties that had a slit down the middle.

"Wear these for me."

She took them in her hand, and went back out to change. She re-emerged very quickly, then she took off his jacket, placed it neatly on the side of the couch and straddled him. He petted her hair and she started to unbutton his shirt. His grey chest hairs sprouted out, and she tugged at the fabric. Awkwardly, he adjusted himself so that she could take his shirt off. She kissed his chest. Lower and lower, she went over him with her mouth until she reached his belt. She knelt down on the floor in front of him. Mr Stevens stood up, undid his belt, unzipped his pants and stepped out of them. Inside his boxer shorts, he was hard.

Kelly stroked his erection. Seductively, she said, "Mmm. What's this?"

"Let me show you," he said, taking off his boxers.

She winked at him and smiled. "You're so big. It looks like you could really hurt me with that."

"I don't want to hurt you, baby," he said. "I won't hurt you. Come here."

She knelt in front of him and took his cock into her mouth. He placed his hands at her head and tugged at her hair until he managed to unravel the bun. It looked as if it hurt. He stroked her hair and looked as though he was in another world, completely devoid of himself and reality.

For a brief moment, I wondered what it would be like for him to drive home to his wife and kids after this, but I didn't care. I didn't know Mr Stevens and, other than a mild curiosity that I have for all strangers, I didn't give a damn. Kelly, on the other hand, was dear to me and I wondered what it did to her to pretend to be okay with this. I wondered what it was like for her to wear that outfit, and to have sex with a man who was old enough to be her father.

She didn't seem disturbed so I let myself indulge in the vision unfolding in front of me.

She paused for air. "Do you like this?"

"Mmm. Yes," he said. "Do you want to come sit on me?"

She nodded.

"I don't want you to take off your panties."

She walked over to him, reached into a jar on the coffee table and pulled out a condom.

"How do you know about these? I thought you were a virgin," he said.

"Stop teasing me."

He split open the package and rolled it onto his cock quickly. Kelly put her hands on his shoulders and slid herself onto him. She made it seem like it hurt a little as she eased herself downward slowly.

"That's my girl. You can take the whole thing, can't you, baby?"

"Mmm." She moaned and bobbed up and down.

It didn't take long for Mr Stevens to come. Not long at all. Kelly was on him for less than five minutes when suddenly his face crinkled and his body stiffened, and he yelped like a little boy.

And that was it. She got off him, patted her outfit straight and sat down next to him, almost as though they were strangers sitting together in their doctor's waiting room.

Mr Stevens sighed. "Thank you, Veronica. It's been a pleasure, as usual."

"Can I get you anything?" she asked.

"No. I should get going."

With that, he got dressed, put on his jacket, took his briefcase and left.

Kelly poked her head behind the divider. "You can come out now."

I didn't say anything. Then Kelly laughed. I laughed.

"Jeez. It takes me longer to put on my eye makeup than it does to get that guy off." She straightened the pillows on the couch. "Come on. I'm going upstairs for a shower. Come with me, and then we can go grab a drink somewhere."

* * * *

"Don't get the impression that it's always that easy," she said from the shower. I sat on the counter in her bathroom and watched, as per her invitation. "I mean, some guys take longer but, you know, for fifteen minutes of my time — if it was even that long — five hundred bucks seems like a fair deal."

She squirted a dollop of facial cleanser into her palms and lathered her face vigorously. She was so beautiful, so graceful and it seemed to come so easily to her. Once out of the shower she towelled off and got out her hair dryer. Her long hair flapped about as she combed parts of it through with a wide-toothed comb.

"A lot of the guys Carla knows will take you out for dinner, or to business functions or whatever, so that's a whole other level of investment."

I wasn't sure what she meant but didn't think I should ask.

"Some of them pay you to stay the night with them in a hotel. So that's kind of challenging, at least for me. I could never sleep or anything."

She took me out to celebrate my new job and her five-minute, five-hundred-dollar evening. We took a cab to a luxury hotel and sat in its lounge, overlooking the city. It was breathtaking.

"See, now, what you wanna do is find someone in a place like this. You know...eventually."

"A man?"

"A rich man," she advised.

"You just have it all figured out, don't you?" I asked.

She looked at me and her tone changed. "I've got nothing figured out. Nothing. I was just making plans for you." Then she laughed.

There was something cryptic about the way Kelly spoke. The things she said never really added up to the whole truth, but then I wondered what the whole truth was. Perhaps some things really were better left unsaid, particularly in new friendships.

That night, back in her apartment, she poured me a bath and sat beside the tub on a towel on the floor while I soaked. She played some bluegrass and bobbed along calmly, quietly.

"I'm glad I met you, Julie," she finally said. "I was getting a little lonely." There was a hint of sadness in her eyes.

"I'm glad I met you, too. Thank you for everything. I'll be out of your hair soon... As soon as Josie leaves, in a few days."

"You're not in the way. I like having you here," she said.

I got up out of the tub after nearly an hour. I was pruny and soft. Kelly passed me a towel and I wrapped it around myself.

"Come on. Let me put some lotion on your back," she said.

I followed her to her bed where she lay me down and massaged my back with pink cream.

"It's peony."

"It's lovely," I purred, absorbing the sensation of her touch.

"Sleep with me, okay?" She kissed the back of my neck. Her lips were so soft they made my neck tingle, and my whole body felt as if I were floating.

"Okay." I turned. She was sitting on the edge of the bed above me. Lying there, looking up at her, I was floored. How had I found someone so beautiful?

She leant down and I sat up a bit. Our lips met and we kissed. It was so gentle and so sweet. I had kissed Tommy, but this was different. We opened our eyes and backed away from each other. Kelly smiled at me and I'm sure I beamed right back.

She crawled into bed, pulled her plush covers over us and turned away from me. I put my arms around her and my legs against the backs of hers. She fell asleep innocently and sweetly, like an angel. I stayed awake a little while. I couldn't shake the thought that I had just kissed a girl, and that it was Kelly, and that she was great and felt so good.

* * * *

I can't say that it was easy to become accustomed to the work. I had no real difficulty with the idea of it. I certainly didn't care much about the religious implications that my mother and sister would have been horrified by. That stuff didn't bother me. What was much harder to take was the monotony of it.

I had barely started and I was bored. Bored. Of sexual talk, flirtation, sexual attention. Everything. It seemed so formulaic with men. I could feel their hearts pounding before I even came into the room. I could practically hear their massive gulps when they saw me. It was so predictable. It was unsatisfying how utterly simple most men were.

I guess when I'd fantasised about my brilliant career, it had included all sorts of exotic perversions. I thought I would be repulsed, titillated, engrossed. I thought I would find fascinating folks with secret lives. But I had been a naïve country girl. These men weren't any more special than the ones back home. They were following convention, having their perfunctory extramarital sex. The single ones were filling their quota, as if taking their vitamins. I had duped myself. The most exciting part about working was the money, the way the cash just kept coming. But the main reason I was there was Kelly. If I left, I wasn't sure how I'd hold onto her and keep her in my life, and I wanted her to stay.

I became more and more enamoured with Kelly. The days melted into each other and I barely paid attention to my work. I lived for the time Kelly and I spent together. It seemed as though she saw something that I didn't. It was as if she had an insight into the profession, or the men, or the setting. Maybe she liked it more than me. Or less. Or maybe she had got past her interest in liking it. Maybe her experience of it was much more profound than a matter of mere liking versus disliking.

Either way, I wanted to learn from her. I wanted her to show me what she knew. I sort of hoped that, by virtue of her showing me, I would see something of her, too. I guess what I really wanted to know was her, but I didn't get that then.

Kelly was generous with her knowledge. She wanted me to sit in on her sessions and was disappointed when I didn't. It started to bother me watching her with men, seeing her eyes glazed over, watching her calculated moves. The more I got to know her, the more I wanted to watch her experience pleasure, not what she called a means to an end. I had been at it for long enough to know what to do and so for me her lessons were redundant — except, of course, for the fact that I wanted to spend as much time with her as possible and I was glad that she allowed me to do that.

Another one of her regular clients, Mr Collis, had been away for a few weeks. He was usually such a regular that he claimed he couldn't go a week without seeing his beloved Mistress Veronica, or at least that was what Kelly told me.

We were in her apartment on a sunny Tuesday morning. Kelly slipped her feet into those shiny boots of hers and donned a tight, black, PVC dress. I helped her lace up the corset portion. Carla had yet to give me any of the submissive clients. They were the coveted bunch, the ones who didn't want sex as much as they wanted to worship feet and get spanked. Kelly had kept those clients sort of discreet, letting me sit in on all her standard sessions but not those ones. For that reason, I was particularly thrilled to be privy to the reunification of Mr Collis and Mistress Veronica.

"It's easier for me to get into this character," Kelly said. "I'm tired of the costume thing. I hate doing the standard stuff. I hate the guys who come here for tenderness. It's like, jeez, get a girlfriend, I don't want to massage you. God."

"Yeah. They always want that."

"In this business, the customer's not always right. In fact, he's almost always wrong. That's what I like about being Mistress Veronica. I get to speak my mind and it's fine. In fact, it's mutually beneficial. Just watch."

I did, and it was amazing.

Mr Collis approached Kelly's room as if he were entering a shrine. He was so careful and considerate. As soon as Kelly opened the door and emerged from the adjacent room, he dropped to his knees and greeted her with a kiss on each boot. She reciprocated with a kick to his face — not a violent kick, but a firm one nonetheless. The room was dimly lit with a few scattered dark red candles. Despite the sunny morning outside, Kelly had made sure to close all the blinds and close the blackout curtains. Kelly said she liked to go all out for Mr Collis because he went all out for her. He always came with a bag full of presents, and not sick stuff like crotchless knickers. Usable, good stuff, like really fancy chocolate truffles, a cashmere scarf or a lovely gold bracelet. One time he bought her a full day spa treatment at one of the most luxurious hotels in San Francisco. Mr Collis was a rich, middle-aged man. According to Kelly, he was a real gentleman.

After kissing her boots and bowing down and thanking her for kicking him in the face, Mr Collis offered Mistress Veronica a foot massage. "Anything to please Mistress. Please forgive me for having been away from you for so long."

"I might forget, but I'll never forgive and you know it," she said.

"May I please caress those gentle, beautiful feet of yours, Mistress?"

Mr Collis sat on the floor while Kelly seated herself like a Persian cat on a throne. He slowly sniffed at and undid the zippers of her boots, carefully brought out her feet and sat there staring at them for a long time, as though he were afraid of touching her. From where I was, behind the divider again, I felt his pain. I, too, would have been afraid to touch such a majestic creature. As Kelly, at night, she was my best friend and I slept in her bed, holding her dearly and tenderly, but in this light she was a goddess and a force beyond my comfort zone.

Mr Collis eventually held her feet, one at a time, in his palms the way one holds fine, antique silk. I couldn't blame him for his zeal. Kelly thrust her toes at him almost as though she were attacking him. She opened his lips and mouth with her big toe and prised her way into him. It was oral pleasure like I'd never seen it before. She was rougher on him with her toes than any man had been on either one of us, and watching how much Mr Collis enjoyed it was more than a little stimulating. My panties dampened inside the dark room as I watched, anxiously anticipating what would happen next.

What happened was beyond what I could have imagined. She became angry with Mr Collis, for not getting her off, she said. Mr Collis apologised profusely. Instead of accepting his supplication, Kelly brought out a leather whip and instructed him to pull his pants down, because she wanted to see his bare skin and teach him how to treat her properly.

He followed the order and she went at him like an angered mother at a busy supermarket. She was relentless, and Mr Collis thanked her and bowed down so that his face was hidden in the carpet. His sounds were muffled but it seemed as though he was crying. It went on and on until finally, twenty minutes later, Kelly seemed as though she was satisfied — or bored — and stopped. He thanked her again and she put her whip down, kicked his ass and told him that he could have relief. She passed him a tissue. He thanked her again and took his cock in his hand. He jerked himself back and forth a little bit, then moaned in pleasure and collected his seed in the tissue in his hand, which he immediately crumpled up and put to one side. He fell forward, deep into the carpet in a final stupor. Kelly looked pleased with herself and sat on the sofa next to him, watching him intently. There was nothing indifferent about her this time. She looked engaged and happy.

Mr Collis dressed himself and said, "Thank you, Mistress Veronica. I've brought you something in the hopes of appeasing you. I understand your anger over my bad behaviour and I promise not to stay away this long again." Then he went to his jacket pocket and pulled out a tiny box.

She opened it. "Diamond solitaire earrings. They're lovely," she said. "But don't think that you can buy my affection."

With that, she took the box and walked away, back into the adjoining room, and closed the door. Mr Collis, stunned, let out a massive sigh, put on his jacket and sat down on the sofa with his face between his knees. He sobbed slightly. I couldn't hear it—I knew because of the way his body jerked ever so delicately and he grasped his legs in a foetal position. After a few minutes, some composure came over him and he got up and left.

Chapter Four

We never locked the bathroom door. I'd only ever had that kind of intimate relationship — where I could sit on the toilet in front of someone — with my sister, and even then I'd resented her presence. Kelly seemed so comfortable in her own skin. She didn't care if she was taking a bath, shaving her legs or her armpits or if she was changing a tampon. I was always welcome in front of her and that felt special.

I had come to the city looking for money, and I'd found it. But I think the novelty of my job would have worn off if it hadn't been for the friendship — or what I then *called* a friendship — with Kelly.

Carla kept me on standard, straightforward clients. One evening a man in his mid-twenties, a well-to-do academic type, came to see me. He wanted to see Josie, actually, but I was the one who met him downstairs in Carla's lounge. I tried to make conversation with him but he was stand-offish, which I thought was strange. Maybe he was just afraid of talking to girls. I reckoned that he had been turned down so often he had become all too familiar with the feeling of pretty girls being mean to him. He was the kind of guy who hadn't danced at the prom.

"I just need to relax," he said, as though I was somehow in his way.

"Okay." I was calm. "Is that something I can help you with?" I winked. Flirty, I thought.

"Listen, you're pretty and I'm sure you want a good tip—and I'll leave you one—just stop talking and massage me." The tension oozed off him and I wanted to kick him out. I wanted to tell him what an idiot I thought he was, but I didn't think Carla would be impressed so I didn't say anything. I kneaded his shoulders and back and thought about what might happen if I just took charge the way Kelly did. Instead, I promised myself a walk along the harbour later. I thought about dying my hair. I thought about how I was going to tell Kelly about him. Half an hour passed with our silent interaction.

Then he turned over on the table and revealed his semi-erection underneath the thin white sheet.

"On second thought," he started, "I changed my mind."

It was perverted. He was an asshole, a spoilt brat. I might have been able to get into it if he had been nice about it, but he didn't think I mattered enough to have to be nice. He thought all he had to do was shell out his money, and any service he desired would follow.

"You changed your mind about what?" I asked. My voice was stern.

"I think I want a little something extra," he said, looking down at his cock.

"Too late."

"What? I thought you wanted a nice tip."

"Oh, I'll get my *nice tip*."

"Honey, you have to earn it," he whispered. He put his hand on my shoulder and vaguely tried to pull my head down.

"Get a girlfriend," I sneered. I could tell he was just the kind of insecure mama's boy who expected that everyone would cower to his wants. Well, not me. And I knew that calling him on it would anger him.

"What the hell is that supposed to mean? I'm a paying customer."

"For a massage. That was what you wanted. You said so yourself." I was prepared to stand behind my statement even to Carla. Nothing was worth being talked to like that. I could walk out on this job and find another.

"That's a bad attitude." His response was so predictable, but his actions surprised me. He grabbed my hair and pulled me towards him, not aware yet that one mustn't take what is not offered. I grabbed his wrist and twisted it.

"Let go of me."

"I could have you fired," he said. "I'd be doing you a favour. You're young. You should go to college or something."

"And how do you know I'm not?" I asked.

"Are you?"

I didn't want to tell him that I wasn't so I didn't say anything. Instead, I decided that I would lose him as a client and I'd be doing him a favour. He couldn't rely on his parents' money forever and this was no way to talk to a lady.

"Here's what's going to happen. You're going to walk out that door and you're going to go down to Carla and tell her that you had the most incredible experience of your life with me, and then you're going to pay twice as much as she tells you to. You're going to insist. And why? Because you learned the most valuable lesson of your life here today. Then you're going to go home and think about what you've learned. You're going to start being good to people and treating women with the respect that we deserve and then, when you've worked it all out, you're going to come back here and tell me about it and maybe, if I believe you, we'll go for dinner — on you, of course — and you can have the pleasure of my acquaintance in public, which I know is actually what you really want."

I was expecting him to flare into a mad frenzy. Anyone with self-respect would. I had insulted him to the core. But, not surprisingly, he did exactly as I said. He got dressed, thanked me and left.

Later that afternoon, Carla knocked on my door. "Here's your first bonus. I don't know what went down in that room, but he couldn't stop raving about you," she said, and smiled. "Nice work. Welcome to your new life."

People who grew up with money either learn this lesson late in life — the so-called 'hard way' — or not at all. Money is not power. Money can't actually buy anything — it's an illusion. If used correctly, it can be powerful. But that makes it no different than anything else. If we were playing a game of cards, that jerk's hand would have been no match for mine, even if he had gone to all the right schools and would eventually become a snooty, high-paid lawyer.

I told Kelly about him — about what a pasty, puffy-lipped dork he'd been. That, I thought, would be his worst nightmare — the threat that a pretty girl, be she paid or not, would recount all his insecurities and laugh at them with her friends. It had to be most men's worst nightmare. It was also to my great advantage, and so I didn't tell Kelly what I had made him do.

Instead, I told her I wanted to take her out. I wanted to reciprocate even just a little of the hospitality she had shown me.

* * * *

We walked from our house through Chinatown to Kelly's favourite restaurant. Sometimes, she said, she got homesick and went to this place that served up the best fried chicken she had managed to find outside Alabama. I didn't have the same kind of attachment to my home. Her childhood, I speculated, had been laced with these kinds of memories — tastes and smells — and she told me her parents had been sad when she'd decided to leave.

"What could I do?" she asked. "They didn't get that Green Hill was a dead end for me. What could I have done there?"

"What did they want?"

"They wanted me to get married, have children, be like them, I guess. But they hated their lives. At least, that's what it looked like to me. I hated my life. Maybe theirs was okay. I never asked. Anyway, I had to get away from my uncles. I had to get away from..." She stopped, looked into a little shop window and tugged on my arm. "Damn, it's closed. I'll have to take you here some time. They have the most amazing things in here."

It was an antique shop with beautiful, old, art deco oak furniture piled high at the back. It was dark now, and I imagined it was the kind of place that was dark even on sunny days because there was so much stuff piled on display.

"Look at that little box." She pointed at the window. Her finger touched the dewy glass and left a mark. It was a gold pill box with gemstones on the top of it. I didn't know if she was really keen on the box or if it was her way of changing the subject, so I never asked about either again.

Her favourite place was an old-style diner that seemed to be in the middle of nowhere. We had walked through a stretch of warehouses and were somewhere in the industrial district, but I was no longer sure exactly where. It's funny what you learn about people based on where they like to eat. When I'd first seen Kelly, I'd thought she was the embodiment of glamour. She'd been everything 'big city' in my mind, but I had been wrong. Green Hill, she said, was a tiny little town, a forty-minute drive from another fairly small town. She had grown up, much like me, obsessing over the idea of a bigger, brighter, better place.

"So, what's your plan? You know…at Carla's?" she asked as we were seated in the blue vinyl booth.

It was a direct question. I had barely moved in. I had almost screwed up with today's client. I didn't even know if I could cut it. "I'm not sure yet." I grabbed the plastic menu and studied it, hoping we weren't going to talk about work all night.

"Well, a word of advice?"

"Sure."

"Carla knows what she's doing. She's a good person, you know? She's the reason I could leave my job at the Side Bar and I'm glad I'm out of that dive. I don't want to do that anymore. It's hard. It was okay when I first got here. It seems like this place is a big city, you know, but it's not. You will get recognised. I didn't think so at first. I couldn't imagine it. But then it happened. I was minding my own business, shopping for groceries and some guy, some random asshole, came up to me and said, 'It's you, isn't it?' and I was like, 'Who?' but we both knew and…"

"You hated it?"

"Hate is a strong word. I'm very private. I don't like knowing people I haven't set out to know. The good thing about Carla's is that it's a lot of regulars, a lot of word of mouth and overall pretty decent people."

"And the bad thing?"

"Money. She takes half of everything. It's not my idea of a good deal. It's just I needed something to get on my feet. She's getting the better end of the stick, though, I'll tell you that much."

"But the other day you said that it was great money."

"In comparison to the Side Bar, but it's not a long-term thing for me. I don't want to get stuck making someone else rich, you know?"

She glanced at the menu. "I'll order for you," she said. "I'm the Southerner. I like this place. Betty-Anne, the owner, really is from the South. It's the real deal here. You like okra?"

"Don't know."

The waitress, a middle-aged woman with a ponytail and a pencil behind her ear, came over. Kelly ordered a ton of food and smiled at me. "Good for the soul," she said, revealing the twang she usually hides to the waitress, who also smiled.

"So what's *your* plan?" I asked.

"Long term, I want to build my own thing. I'm not sure what yet. I'm not even sure if I'll stay in this industry. It can really wear you out if you're not careful."

"You seem pretty together."

"How do you mean?" Her question was vaguely defensive, as if she didn't like that I had made that observation.

"I just mean that you seem to be pretty happy."

"Yeah, well, 'seem' is the word there."

"Really?" It hit me. I don't know what kind of strange vision of Kelly I'd carried around in my head before that moment. I had sincerely thought that she liked what she did. I had been naïve, I guess.

"You were so nice to me. I guess I thought you were happy." I knew it was a dumb thing to say.

"So being nice is being happy?" Kelly retorted. I didn't blame her. I was nervous and I've always had a bad habit of saying dumb things when I get nervous.

"That's not what I meant." I didn't know how to take it back. I didn't know what to say. I had hurt her feelings because of my own stupidity. God, I just wanted to hold her and tell her I was sorry and for her to forgive me. Her eyes were piercing, as if she had a threshold that, once crossed, would make her turn harsh and angry almost immediately. "Sorry, it's just that you're the one that asked me to stay at Carla's. I thought you..."

"You wanted my help, remember?"

"I'm sorry, Kelly."

"Look, forget it. If you want my advice, marry rich. It's the easiest way. Self-preservation, security. You're not cut out for this."

I was insulted and hurt. I didn't know what to say. I hadn't expected her to be so blunt and I couldn't make myself come back with anything.

Our food arrived and we didn't broach the subject of my career again. All along, though, behind our surface conversation, I kept returning to her statement. I couldn't figure out if she was trying to be nice to me —

'self-preservation'? — or if it was her way of telling me that she didn't think I was good enough. If she really meant it was the easiest way, why wasn't she on the lookout for herself?

* * * *

It was mid October, and I couldn't get the jerk's comment out of my mind that I should do something with my life and go to school. Did I really want to be doing this forever? The answer was no. Solidly. I was bored. I also couldn't get Kelly's statement out of my head. It was mean, like something my family would tell me. Marrying rich wasn't what I wanted. If I'd wanted that, I could have just stayed in bloody Glendale and married some Idaho tycoon and sprouted out kids. How could she even have said that to me?

I wanted to have as much of an idea of where I was going as Kelly had. On my days off, I browsed the bookstores for information. I hadn't grown up with the idea of going to college but that shouldn't stop me. I hadn't even taken SATs because, well, why would I? I wasn't particularly good at school, even though my dad had said I was smart as a whip.

I bought a study guide and took it home. I perused the pages and read all of the words carefully. At first none of it made sense but, once I forced myself to sit down with that book for an hour a day, I found myself retaining the oddest information and actually enjoying reading the newspapers and magazines that Carla subscribed to. She was different from us, that was for sure. She seemed so accustomed to this lifestyle, as if it were just the most natural thing in the world to live in a beautiful house in Berkeley. I still couldn't leave the front door without feeling as though I had somehow landed in the lap of luxury. What was so bad about giving a few blow jobs to earn my keep here? And that thought, I knew, was the fundamental difference between Carla and me.

Here I was, miles away from where I came from, having simple interactions, all things I had done with Tommy. I wasn't convinced that Carla wanted me to feel comfortable as much as I was convinced that she wanted to sell me to the highest bidder. Kelly was right about her — she was smart.

But so were we. One of Kelly's regular patrons had been waiting for the opportunity of two girls at once to come along. Josie, for whatever reason, had declared early on that she wasn't into it. Kelly had arranged for him, Mr Rutherford, to take us to a hotel and pay us directly without Carla's knowledge.

Our job was to interact and fulfil Mr Rutherford's desires. I embraced the principle of the task. Kelly, who knew him best, was to direct me and I would follow his orders. I never saw it as the financial opportunity it was, nor did I see it as servitude to Mr Rutherford. I really just did it the way I would have done absolutely anything for Kelly. We took a cab to the hotel, Kelly feeling smug about the whole arrangement.

"We've gotta start doing this more. This is our ticket out of Carla's. You know, we could just fuck Carla, leave that house, get an apartment together and work like this all the time."

"I suppose so." I don't know why I was hesitant. I guess when I thought about living with Kelly, which I did quite often, I pictured us each having moved on somehow. I pictured her wearing a loose, thin linen shirt and painting in our living room. I pictured coming home to her. I didn't picture the two of us going out to meet Mr Rutherford. But here we were and it wasn't bad at all. In fact, I was prepared to have my socks knocked off. I had never been in a fancy hotel room. And even though I had watched Kelly many times, I had never actually participated.

She approached Mr Rutherford, who was waiting for us in the room, with her usual ease—made a bit of small talk, offered him a cup of tea as a joke. We all laughed. Though he had arranged this for her hospitality, tea was the last thing on his mind.

Then Kelly immersed herself in his world. As though she could read his mind, she took her shirt off, revealing a tight corset underneath. She ordered me to remove my clothes—all of them—immediately. I did as I was told. I wouldn't dare disappoint Mistress Veronica, whose tone and delivery were so skilled. I was to be her assistant and I wanted nothing more than to do the best possible job. Naked, I knelt by her as she gestured for me to do. We were mere inches from where Mr Rutherford sat on the king-size hotel room bed. Kelly took me by my hair so quickly that I let out a gasp. When she grabbed me this way, it was sexy. It told me I was in good hands. I wanted her to take charge, to hold on to me however she saw fit.

She kissed me while watching Mr Rutherford. Her tongue pierced into my mouth as she held me with one hand. It wasn't the soft kissing I was used to at night. This was ferocious, and everything I had imagined about Mistress Veronica. With her free hand, she caressed my breasts until my nipples were hard, then she stood up quickly, pulling me with her and forcing me, by my hair, to place my nipple in Mr Rutherford's mouth.

The sensation of his eager sucking went straight through me and my excitement dripped out of me. Held by Mistress Veronica and nibbled on by this older, almost startled gentleman, I was ready to do anything with them. I loved the attention the combination gave me. Mr Rutherford moaned as though he was the luckiest man alive, and I understood the sound with ease. Mistress Veronica unzipped his pants and held my head down to take his cock into my mouth. I complied, both because I had no choice and because there was nothing I wanted more than to see what she would think of next. I hoped she would force me onto Mr Rutherford's cock, if only to appease my yearning clit.

She used my mouth to harden him and just as I thought she was going to mount him in front of me, she merely sat on his lap instead, facing me. Her back to him, she took my hand and guided my mouth to her lovely, moist cunt. I wanted to devour her. She rose up and started writhing her way down his hard shaft. Both of them moaned. He put his arms around her, cupping her breasts and fingering her nipples, and her eyes stayed locked with mine the whole time.

I sensed what she wanted and licked her with him inside her. She leant back on him, exposing more of her pussy for me. She spread her legs wide. I licked at her swollen pinkness and, even more so than with Tommy, I felt the sensation that I wanted more and more of her. I couldn't get enough. She started to slide up and down rhythmically, almost jumping. Her breasts bounced beautifully and she moaned with delight as her body shivered with a powerful orgasm.

I was in awe. I had never seen anything so seductive. It was different from what men did. I wanted to explore more of her, but she changed position. Her attention turned towards him...and me. He was massive, much bigger than he had been in my mouth. His eyes were large with disbelief. I wondered if she had ever climaxed with him before, or whether this was a special offering for me that had nothing to do with him. I chose to believe the latter. Just as I chose to believe that she was the one fucking me when she took me by my hair again, slid her fingers to my opening and guided me, slowly, onto Mr Rutherford's glistening cock. He tried to grab my hips and thrust inside me, but Mistress Veronica slapped him on the side of his face.

"This isn't about you. It's our first time together so, if you don't mind, have the decency to be patient and we'll make it worth your while." She didn't give him a choice in the matter.

He complied with gratitude, leaning back and stroking my skin gently. "Whatever you like, Veronica. I'm just glad to be here."

"It's Mistress Veronica to you," I said to him. "And she's about to fuck me with your cock so if you don't mind..."

"Sorry," he said, cupping my ass with his palms and letting us share the moment I'd been waiting for weeks to experience. He wasn't in the way, though. I actually liked having his shocked face behind me. Picturing his expression was a huge turn-on for me, probably because I was equally shocked and pleased and in suspense.

Kelly placed a soft cushion in front of me and knelt down where I sat, straddling Mr Rutherford's cock. She brought her tongue closer and I could feel her saliva lubricating his shaft, making it easier for me to ease onto him. Her breath provided a rhythmic slowness that I needed, and I lowered myself completely and felt him stretch me in a way that I had wanted. Kelly was gentle and caressed me sweetly, which was pleasant and almost sentimental. For a moment, it seemed as though she slipped out of the Mistress Veronica character and touched me with the kind of tenderness specific to Kelly. I wanted this terribly and maybe I just imagined it. I wanted to see her as taking me.

I lifted myself up and down and watched as Kelly licked my clit. Forcefully, I did exactly as she had done, pounding myself onto him harder and harder. He said he couldn't take it any longer, held my hips in place and shoved himself deep inside me. He pulled out just in time to release his hot liquid all over my back. Then he sighed in utter relief and rested himself against the pillows propped up on the bed. Normally, this is where a session would have ended, the male climax being the most coveted of moments, but Kelly took me and tossed me onto the other bed in the room, as though Mr Rutherford were out of the picture completely.

"I want you to come," she said.

Her words went straight to my clit and I almost felt myself tremble just at the sound of them. On the bed, I lay flat on my back and Kelly forced my legs apart and massaged my pussy with her tongue. She gave me the gentle touch I longed for. Back and forth, up and down she went until a massive explosion built within. I felt it surface, felt the world disappear once more as I gasped for air and felt my heartbeat race. Then waves of bliss came crashing over me. Kelly stayed with me, holding me.

I felt triumphant. Kelly kissed me again and I kissed her back as best I could. It was my way of showing my dedication to her. She had done everything right.

That night, Kelly and I each made Mr Rutherford come once more, which resulted in a heavy bonus. I knew from the start of the evening that any money we received would pale against the satisfaction of experiencing Kelly. A couple of hours later, we took a cab home and stopped off at the convenience store for instant noodles and fashion magazines. We stayed in her suite and slept together in her bed. She cradled me and held me from behind. I slept soundly against her.

* * * *

Sometimes, sitting at my dresser, applying powder to my face to cover the redness the last client had left in preparation for the next, I'd make eye contact with myself and, for a brief moment, picture myself at law school, or medical school, or business school. Then working at an office and taking care of Kelly, providing everything she needed. She wanted to be an artist, she'd told me once, while drunk, then had never spoken of it again.

One evening, while we were hanging out in Kelly's suite casually painting our toenails and flipping through magazines, as though we were just like the sorority girls on campus, I tried to tell her how I felt.

"You know what, Kelly? Sometimes I just feel so grateful for knowing you."

"Aw, thanks, sugar." She smiled. "Hey, what do you think of this colour?" She held up a peachy pink opalescent nail polish.

I nodded. Talking about feelings is hard at the best of times. What had I been thinking, anyway? Kelly loathed that kind of thing. The closest I could ever come to her was sleeping with her.

That night, when she crawled into bed with me, I kissed her. It wasn't like the other time — the gentle, innocent time. And it wasn't the over-the-top, exaggerated kisses she'd given me for Mr Rutherford's benefit. It was better. It was firm, juicy and real. It was the way I had kissed Tommy, but more intense.

Although she seemed to enjoy it, too, she pulled away. "What are you doing? There's no one but us here."

It was heartbreaking, though I didn't realise it at the time. I just felt awkward and clammy, as if I had done something really bad. The thing about Kelly was that she naturally called all the shots. She could do whatever she wanted. But it didn't work that way for me. She looked at me quizzically, and I didn't know what I could do.

"Sorry," I said, and got out of her bed. I went to the bathroom for solace. I didn't know what I had been expecting. Was it sex? Was that what I wanted? Well, the short answer was a resounding 'yes', but the long answer was harder to fathom. Would we then be a couple? Would we do what normal couples did and build a life together, and buy a house together and all that stuff I'd loathed so much back in the Tommy days? I didn't loathe thinking about doing all that stuff with Kelly. But it was pretty clear that she wasn't thinking of me in that way.

I sat on the toilet and cried. Part of me hoped she would come to the washroom and get me, and take me to her bed, and comfort me. Another part of me didn't want her to know I was crying.

I slept in my own bed that night, and every subsequent night thereafter. Like all the other things we never spoke about, we buried that kiss in a secret abyss. We didn't do more evenings with Mr Rutherford.

I couldn't quit this job for another month without getting a heavy penalty from Carla. Kelly and I kept to ourselves after that. We still greeted each other and were congenial, but I had managed to kill the one thing I wanted more than anything else.

My priorities shifted. I couldn't wait to move on. I told Carla that I would be leaving at Christmas and that I'd help her find someone to replace me. She didn't seem surprised. Then I pocketed as much money as I could and kept it in a savings account. I didn't know what I would get up to after that. It was enough of a challenge, at that point, just to get through the days and nights.

School finally let out mid December, and I was free to go without destroying Carla's precious illusion.

On the morning I left, Kelly came and knocked on my door. It was a strange sound, since we had been accustomed to leaving our doors open and, during that last month, just not talking. I opened the door and she came in and sat on my bed, next to my suitcase.

"So this is it, huh?"

"I don't know. You tell me." I was surprised by my own attitude.

"Well, you're leaving, aren't you?"

"Yeah, well, so are you, sooner or later. So what?"

"Well, Merry Christmas to you, too." She shot down my belligerence with her more refined sarcasm.

"Kelly, what do you want?" I asked, straight out.

"I don't know." Her eyes were teary and she looked apologetically at me, even though I felt as if it was me who should apologise.

"I don't want it to end like this," I said.

She stood up and hugged me. We embraced for several minutes. Her hair smelt so familiar and so right to me, and I couldn't understand what I was doing leaving her behind. I couldn't go on and live my life without her, but I couldn't stay here and work it out with her either. What was there to work out? What could I possibly say to her?

"Take care of yourself, okay?" she whispered.

"I will. You, too."

"You know I will," she said.

We both kind of laughed, but not really. It was the saddest goodbye I'd ever experienced. I'd felt no remorse leaving the farm I'd lived on my whole life, but leaving the room across the hall from Kelly's, where I'd been for three months, made me break down and cry. But not until I'd reached the comfort of my hotel room, where I knew I was safe and alone.

Chapter Five

San Francisco, again

I knew I would miss Kelly terribly. But I also knew that I would see her again. I knew that in a parallel universe we could be lovers, and that I might eventually convince her to come with me if I carved out the right situation for us. If not, she had also taught me—and would therefore understand better than anyone—that my own needs were foremost.

I took a cab to the most exclusive hotel I knew about, had the attendant bring up my bags and paid, for the first time, for my own comfort. My room was luxurious and I decided that I would become accustomed to such luxury immediately. The farm was a world away and now Carla's would be, too. I would not go back to the house. I was, after all, in the constantly changing and opportunistic world of plentiful gifts and trinkets. I knew how to get what I wanted on all accounts, except with Kelly.

I stayed in bed the first night, feeling as if I didn't have a friend in the world. It felt like starting over again. It felt as though I had just arrived in San Francisco and didn't know anyone.

I knew that, if I was going to survive this, I would have to thicken my skin, toughen up and move on. I couldn't afford to dwell on possibilities. I had come here to make a life for myself and I was closer than ever. I had more money than I ever could have imagined in Idaho. I had a whole new set of skills and I had an extensive wardrobe to go with them.

The next day, I went shopping. I was determined to find a rich man to marry.

It's a strange goal to set for yourself, but at the time it seemed my only option and, for that reason, I made it a good option. I ordered a cappuccino at the hotel, drank it slowly while reading the paper, and looked around for successful-looking men. Then I left the lounge and wandered up and down the streets, stepping into the fancy clothing stores. If this was my plan, I would have to look the part.

That evening, dressed in my decadent new dress and upholstered with my false yet realistic eyelashes, I sauntered to the bar in the lobby where I not only belonged, but radiated. All eyes were on me as I entered the candlelit room, found myself a little table against the back wall and waited for a suitor.

"May I join you?" was the first question the older gentleman asked.

I didn't answer. I preferred to keep him uncertain and offered, instead, a small smile and a gesture to the adjacent lounge chair. Men are easy — sometimes extremely easy — to read. I looked him up and down. Without so much as an exchange of names or pleasantries, I pictured him like a cut of meat — sized, wrapped, garnished. From slaughter to serving dishes, I knew his sexual history and desires as if I had been along for every turn in every road. It was child's play to me.

I ran my fingertips up and down my wet martini glass. He tried not to look, tried not to be affected, but he had been mine since he'd walked into the room.

"Where are you from?" I asked.

"Virginia." If he had still been wearing a hat, he would have tipped it to me. His manners were impeccable, and his three-piece suit suggested not just money but old, conservative wealth. He looked like the kind of boy who had grown up on a parallel farm to my own but who hadn't had to labour—who had been fawned over instead. He had grown up watching strapping young lads haul stacks of hay and plough through his overgrown fields, standing on his porch, unsure of why he was so titillated watching them.

The Southern gentleman is a girl's best friend. He wants the appearance of something sweet and wholesome. What this man wanted more was one of the chiselled men to take him, rough as they are with their equipment, and force him into submission. I don't know how I became capable of seeing these things, but there was no point in questioning it. This, absolutely, was the beginning of a beautiful friendship. I introduced myself.

"The city is so beautiful and magical," I said. "It would be lovely to see it from high above."

"If you don't mind the suggestion, Miss Julie, you would be more than welcome to enjoy the view from my suite on the sixteenth floor."

"Why, Mr Broughton, are you suggesting that I visit the suite of a man I barely know?"

"Forgive me. I have been too forward. My intentions are pure."

Perhaps they were. It wasn't an outright lie. He seemed interested in the company of the fairer sex. I could easily slip into his life like gold cuff links, an extravagant adornment for him to show off to the world. Whether I was the centre of his fantasies or not, he had something that was at the centre of mine.

"I am supposed to leave tomorrow. I'm catching a train back to New York." I tested his dedication to what might be our mutual cause.

"Oh, what a shame. Is it urgent?"

"Not at all."

"Then might I suggest that I rent the other suite for you on the sixteenth floor, and you stay here with me for a few days so that we may become better acquainted?"

"Why, that sounds lovely." We clinked glasses. And with that I knew he was not only honourable, but also ready to indebt himself to me.

Mr Broughton—Hal—was an old-world gentleman, the kind I'd only heard of, never witnessed. He could have dropped straight out of the stories—he was handsome, powerful and charming. Just as in the stories, I imagined the nuances of complicated love affairs, family complications and career catastrophes. He struck me as the kind of man women would fawn over, melt in front of and do anything for. I think I projected these traits onto him because, even at first, he was only ever forthright with me. For all of his worldliness, he was the most mild-mannered, soft-spoken man I could imagine. It was almost a shame that he'd landed in my lap as untainted as he was, but I think it worked out well for both of us. He would have followed me like a lost puppy. Good thing I was ready to take the lead.

After a lovely evening of wine and bourbon and animated conversation, I moved to the room next to his, this time overlooking an even more spectacular view of the city. The next morning, he begged my acquaintance again.

"I would love to join you for dinner tonight, but I'm afraid you've already seen me in my one pretty dress. I wasn't anticipating staying in the city." I was on my best behaviour. It's no secret that you never get more than what you ask for.

"Say no more, my dear." He opened his pocketbook and pulled out more bills than I had ever held in my hands. "I'll meet you at five in the lobby for martinis."

"I'll look forward to it." I winked.

With that, I was off for a day of shopping at the best boutiques. Nothing but the most extravagant would do. I started from the inside and worked out, buying myself a black velvet corset and panties with frills. It was the kind of luxury that Carla would have envied. I had my long hair styled and indulged in a manicure and pedicure. This was the life I had wanted when I left home and now, only days after leaving Carla's house, it was mine. I gathered it could stay my reality forever, from the sound of Hal's voice. Women are loved the way they want to be loved, and I owned Mr Hal Broughton.

In the lounge, to the outside observer, it might have appeared as though I was my companion's plaything. Mr Broughton's salt-and-pepper hair and oversized belly emanated experience. The lines around his eyes and mouth indicated a rich life of laughter and money, but I saw something others were unaware of. Hal suffered. It was clear from his milky white hands that he'd been privy to the kind of nepotism that makes a man soft. He had no clue what his role was. His accomplishments had been orders that he had filled out. His whole life had been lived for approval. Yes, this was a man who was so out of touch with his own desires, so far removed from his inner sexual bully, that he had become a puppet of his parents' fortunes. Taking him would be easy.

We feasted, drank wine, ate fine cheese plates and salads, and he became more and more enamoured as I looked into his eyes with compassion.

"You sure are a lovely creature, Miss Julie," he offered on several occasions. Each time I wondered whether he knew that 'creature' was the operative word. If he didn't, then he would soon find out.

"Mr Broughton, would you care to join me in my room tonight?"

"I would like that very much." His words spilt out of him, delighted as he was that such a beautiful young woman was taking interest in him. Real interest.

"Then you shall be my guest. I am an excellent hostess."

"I'm sure you are."

* * * *

We ordered nightcaps to be sent to my room. A martini for me, and bourbon for Mr Broughton. I lit the candles I'd bought. "I'm going to slip out of this dress and into something more comfortable," I said, eyeing the shopping bags in my boudoir.

"Wait." He paused. "Why don't you come sit next to me for a moment." I joined him on the dark green velvet chaise longue. "It's just that you look so lovely tonight, refulgent and full of energy. I'm…"

We both knew what he was about to say. "I'm...
Well, let's just say I'm from a different generation than
you."

"Why, Mr Broughton! Do you think I'm trying to
seduce you?"

"Heavens, no. Absolutely not," he said. "Heaven
forbid, my goodness."

"Because I'm not. I'm a lady."

"You are an extraordinary lady, Miss Julie — the best
I have ever had the pleasure of knowing."

"Why, thank you. And you are a gentleman. The
best I have known."

"Come with me, Miss Julie."

"What?"

"I mean it. Come with me. You and me. I'd like very
much for you to join me." He took my hands into his
soft, doughy ones.

"Join you? Where?"

"Everywhere. I'm leaving in a week, sailing with my
friend Timothy to Florida. From there I'll be taking a
plane back to Virginia. If you like it there, you're
welcome to stay with me. I mean, if that's okay with
you."

"That's quite an offer. I barely know you. I have my
home in New York City."

"We can send for your things."

"I'll have to think about it. This is very sudden," I
lied. There was nothing to think about. I didn't have a
home. I didn't have things. I had no prospect of ever
having things without working very hard for them.
This was as easy as smearing warm butter on toast.

I approached him, sitting on the chaise. I lunged
onto him, straddling his lap and slipping my legs
around him. My long velvet gown fell onto the floor
and my breasts heaved out of the neckline. He stared

at me in utter amazement. One would think that women do this all the time, but I don't think Mr Broughton had ever experienced this kind of aggression, or even admission that I was ready for him to take me. I was ready to take him. He was overwhelmed. I liked it that way. I always have. I enjoyed total annihilation of self-control and abandonment of social niceties for the sake of utter passion.

Hal was not concurrent.

"Miss Julie," he whispered as I licked his neck, "It's late. Perhaps I'd best be going. I wouldn't want to take advantage of a lady's hospitality."

It was hard to believe him. He had hung on to my words since he'd met me. He was fascinated with me — smitten, even. I was definitely a coveted prize and I was ready to offer myself on a platter. But it was more of a test than anything. Hal, like most men, was so afraid, so intimidated that he didn't know what to do. I'd seen it all the time at Carla's. Men are supposed to have a ferocious sexual appetite. Get them into a room with me who will do anything to fulfil their fantasy because I sincerely enjoy it, and they become little children who need their mothers.

I was hanging off one such man, had my tongue on his neck and my hands around his back and was stroking him in all the right ways. Now he didn't know what to do and it angered me. I think it angered me because the trend had been so prevalent. I supposed that was the difference between the men I saw as clients and the kinds of men who wandered the world and didn't have to make arrangements with a call girl. I had become an expert at dealing with the men least likely to fend for themselves in the sexual realm. If this had been a jungle, I would have been a vicious lioness and the men who saw me, including Hal, would be timid antelope. But if he thought I was going to go along with him, he would have to be prepared for me to test the merchandise. After all, there were dozens of rich men at my disposal and I certainly wouldn't have difficulty meeting others.

"Mr Broughton, stay a while. Get comfortable. I insist."

"But..."

"Really. It would be my pleasure to have you." With that, I took his soft hand and guided it underneath my skirt to my awaiting moisture. He touched my warm pussy and a rush came over me. I took his hand and moved it around in tiny circles, hoping that he would take the opportunity to become more stern. I was more than willing. He looked baffled. Almost on the verge of mortified, as though this had been the last thing on his mind and that I had somehow choreographed the most atrocious humiliation for him, he politely retracted his hand. Had this happened to any woman but me, I'm sure she would have felt forever sullied by his bashful glance. But I wasn't.

* * * *

Just as Kelly had gained the upper hand when she'd rejected my advances, I became intrigued with Hal's convoluted desires. To really win him over, I would have to play his game and, in this case, he wanted desperately to see me as an unattainable lady. I was his fine young prize and he would treat me as such, providing for me the way his wealthy background dictated.

The week passed. I spent my days in extravagance. Hal was busy working, he claimed. There was some trouble with his estate, I gathered from his cryptic descriptions of daily activities. He was in the process of claiming his inheritance, hence the trip to Virginia. It turned out that, despite the occasional hint of a Southern accent, he had only been raised at the manor in Virginia part-time, having spent his childhood being carted back and forth between Europe's finest boarding schools and his grandparents' home in Canada.

Though he travelled freely between all the countries he loved, he explained, inheriting property was a messy matter and his papers weren't clean.

I knew almost immediately that his motivation in San Francisco was twofold. The gentleman needed a wife. This was not a matter of want, but an issue of doing the right thing, as his ageing benefactor had recently become rather opinionated in the decision-making process.

Why, I wondered, had this handsome, eligible man put off marriage for so long? It seemed a mystery to me until I saw the whole situation with absolute clarity. Hal had not spent the last week as a gentleman courting a lady. He had as much interest in ladies as I had in Idaho. We were hardwired that way and, for the first time, I didn't look into Hal's eyes with the intention of dissecting him, as I did with most men. Instead, I looked at him with sincere compassion.

That fate had brought us together was a beneficent realisation.

The most luxurious week of my life came to a sudden close that climaxed with an evening of caviar and pâté in his suite. Hal, once I understood him, was the most entertaining man I'd ever known.

That last night marked the culmination of sizing each other up for the roles we needed each other to play for the next phase of our lives.

"Would you like to be my guest in Virginia?" Hal was blunt after the first few cocktails. I'd waited for the question since the first night he'd made the suggestion. I'd been working on the best possible answer.

I looked out of the window. "I'm sorry, Hal, I'm just not sure about it. I do like you and your offer is tempting, but think about what I might be giving up."

"I don't want you to have to sacrifice. I don't want you to want for anything. Whatever you want, name it and it's yours."

"Lovers."

"What?"

"I want lovers. I want to be able to socialise with whomever I want." I certainly wouldn't be able to tolerate a sexless life of ladylike behaviour. I would only have set myself up for the worst kind of failure.

His face went pale. Perhaps he had been expecting that I would say I wanted a diamond or a driver or an elaborate allowance. Sexuality was just not something that one discussed with Hal. He was a gentleman through and through, and he had no interest in publicising the private.

"That's only fair," he whispered. "After all, I'm..."

"You're what?"

"I'm afraid to tell you."

"Don't be afraid, Hal."

"Well, I'm not young anymore. I just can't..."

He blushed, became unbelievably shy and awkward as he looked into the glass he swivelled elegantly in his hand. I vowed never to discuss the matter again. I hated causing him such discomfort.

"You are a handsome and successful man. I would be proud to be on your arm."

"Really?"

"Yes, yes and yes."

"Oh, Julie, you make me so happy." He kissed my cheek. And with that we sealed our understanding. "I'll do this right, Julie, I assure you. I'll do this the old-fashioned way, the Southern way. You'll want for nothing, I promise you that. If it's lovers you want, well... You'll have the best selection of everything. If it's clothes, or jewellery, or travel, or..."

"Oh, Hal, stop."

"I mean it, Julie. In all my forty-six years, I have never met a woman like you. You understand me. You know what I need. Do you have any idea what that's worth to a man?"

For a moment, I had a difficult time believing Hal, but I knew that I couldn't afford to think that way. Success has no room for self-doubt, and my success was contingent on his acceptance of me. Like Hal, I also had never met anyone like me. I was more than a pretty face—I'm sure he had had his pick of Southern belles before me—and what he saw in me must have been something quite extraordinary, something to do with my wild education and unabashed attitude. Yet I was, to my own surprise sometimes, very much a lady. It was a combination of manners, of my feigned gentility and my obscene mind coalescing somehow with his combined tact and pragmatism. And if he wanted to marry me and give me the life I craved, well, why get in the way of that kind of progress?

"Well, then, ask me properly, Hal."

"What?"

"If I mean that much to you, then ask me properly. I am, after all, a lady and I deserve the kind of propositioning that makes a girl blush."

"Miss Julie, I see there's a bit of a romantic in you, after all."

"If I'm going to marry a Southern gentleman, I have to at least know how to blend in, don't I? Besides, what do you want me to answer when folks ask about your proposal? You wouldn't want a lady to have to lie to defend your honour, would you?"

"Absolutely not."

"Okay then, so I'll expect my wedding proposal in the next few days. Goodnight, Hal." I kissed him on the cheek and left his room.

Back in the comfort of my own suite, I thought about how this could work. *Always an innovator*, I said to myself, over and over. It wasn't so much that I had ever fallen into the right situation—I just seemed to know how to mould situations and work them to my advantage. This would be no different from Carla's.

Except, of course, that it would be the complete opposite. I wondered how much I would even see Hal. I wondered what would happen after my end of the contract was fulfilled. There were many things to negotiate and Hal was not the kind of man to be upfront about his needs.

I'm not a romantic. I have always relied on my rationality and I like it that way. Men are a means to an end. I was his public tart and he was my ladder to climb. I appreciated the soft steps I could take on him and I soon figured out, much to my surprise, that I was capable of loving him. I was capable of finding sincere satisfaction in our agreement and our mutual admiration. I was no more at his mercy than he was at mine and we both knew it. This marriage would be built on understanding, contracts, discretion and fun. I still believe that we had unlocked the secret to marital bliss. It was in exact opposition to conventional definitions of marriage. We would not consummate, would not expect to find sexual satisfaction with each other. Instead, we would become excellent fakers for the cause. I would help him with his secret life and he would give me everything I longed for. We would not have couple friends over for drinks and talk incessantly about how similar we are, the way most married couples do. Instead, we would have carefully selected collaborators who understood us and how they fitted into the scheme of our union.

* * * *

I had a hunch that one such collaborator would be Timothy. Hal had told me of him from the beginning, and always with a slightly upturned lip or a hint of a blush. Giving indication is the easiest thing in the world. Reading it is something else altogether, and I did not know Mr Hal Broughton well enough to read him thoroughly, but if I had seen any indications thus far it was at the mention of Mr Timothy Dappler.

Unlike Hal, who had been born into his gentility, Timothy was a self-made man. According to Hal, Tim was stern, fierce and had the business sense of a stock market tycoon. But that was not the sense I got of him. When I first met Mr Timothy Dappler, in the lobby, I thought he was a charlatan.

"Good day, fine folks," Timothy said, standing up and proffering his hand to greet me. He looked at Hal. "This must be your lovely lady." He brought my hand to his mouth. "It's a pleasure to meet you."

As he kissed my skin, I sensed there was something a little strange about this man. Had it not been for Hal's overwhelming accolades, I might have dismissed my feeling as the kind of disinterested distance I project onto everyone. I had anticipated liking Timothy, which made it worse when I didn't.

"Yes, this is my girl," Hal said. "She'll be travelling back with us and coming to live with me at Strawberry Hill."

"I see. Very good, then," Timothy said. He turned on his heels and snapped his fingers at the bellboy, who promptly picked up Timothy's heavy luggage and followed him outside, not unlike a well-trained pet. And Timothy, who was apparently as lofty as he was successful in his ventures, seemed to revere the attention a little too much.

Hal, bless his heart, appeared to notice nothing. He kissed my cheek, threw his lightweight coat over his shoulder and held his arm out for me. "Shall we?"

Now that I was staring at my future head on, I couldn't help but wonder if I would ever come across as awful and pretentious as Timothy did. I reckoned that the fact that I was asking this question of myself would make it harder for me to be as much of an ill-mannered jerk. Money changes people. It was the one thing Hal had never had to learn, and I was grateful on his behalf.

Chapter Six

At Sea

On board the yacht, Timothy, Hal, and myself enjoyed a staff of three—a captain, a first mate and a cook who would also double as server. It was to be just us all the way to Florida and I was well equipped. Hal had given me money to shop with, and I'd brought with me a full wardrobe and everything I wanted. I also knew what Hal wanted. What they both wanted, and I was the catalyst.

I could tell that Timothy thought of himself as having a similar nature to Hal. Timothy wanted to be genteel with a penchant for the finer things in life. His wife, who lived in South Carolina, was at home—kept, undoubtedly, by a similar deal to my own. If she understood her husband's ways, I would be impressed. I guessed that she did not, given the way Timothy described her and how happy he seemed to be away from her for this sailing vacation. He said she took no interest in being out on the sea. I figured she probably took more interest in having her share of visitors at home. But this was pure speculation on my part.

I warmed up to Timothy only after I realised that I should feel no kinship with his wife. The unfortunate part of being a woman is that it often leads to empathising with other women, simply because of their gender. What did I know of Timothy's wife, and who was I to take offence on her behalf?

Wives have had a bad reputation for generations. It didn't seem unkind of Timothy to be suspicious of Hal's new bride to be. If anything, there was a camaraderie to it that pleased me. And I had to forgive poor Timothy—he had no idea whom he was dealing with.

I started to obsess about their relationship, positioning myself as an agent. Could I facilitate this union between two awkward characters, who had each been raised to believe they were at fault whenever they felt any kind of passion? I would rise to the challenge that this companionship presented. I didn't have to do anything about the dynamic I'd observed. I could easily have contented myself with my own hand and forgotten all about the pleasure of these two, but there we were at sea, alone, and the idea of it titillated me so much that I decided to do it for my own enjoyment. I confronted Timothy while Hal was in the bunk room, having a nap.

"You're quite a lady," Timothy said to me on the deck one night as the sun was going down. "Hal is lucky to have you."

"No one *has* anyone," I responded.

With that, somewhat predictably, Timothy came too close to me and put his hands around me. "You're telling me that I don't have you right now?" he said, with a firm grip around my waist.

"That is what I'm telling you." I ripped his palms from my hips, moved back and stared him down. I would win this awkward battle.

"Oh, Julie," he chuckled. "Don't be so alarmed. I'm sure you're on familiar footing."

"Familiar?"

"I know the kind of woman you are. And, believe me, I'm not against it. How do you think I've made my marriage last all these years?" He winked with the kind of confidence befitting a man who had made his fortune in a dubious way.

"Mr Dappler, I'm afraid you have me mistaken."

"Oh, come on, Julie. You and Hal and this hoax of a relationship. You met him less than two weeks ago and you expect me to believe you're here for anything other than his pocketbook?"

"Why are you here, Timothy?"

"What?"

"You heard me. Why are you here? I don't believe I am the only one interested in Hal's pocketbook."

"I resent that. You have no idea what you're talking about, whore."

"Please. You're not as self-made as you claim. I call your bluff, Mr Timothy Dappler. Who's the real whore here?"

"How dare you?" he whispered as he grabbed my wrist. He gripped me and I felt a sensation I was unfamiliar with. Part of me wanted to yield to this man. Part of me wanted him to call me a whore and take me over his knee and spank me. Another part of me wanted the reverse of that scenario.

It was painfully quiet between us as Hal slept. Was this what had made me sceptical of Timothy when I had first met him? That he had some kind of power over me? I had called his bluff but he had admitted to nothing. Perhaps his lies were worse than I had imagined. Or maybe he knew that Hal and I were never going to be the husband and wife team that Hal had superficially made us out to be. Maybe he liked this about me, and I liked that he accepted me. Maybe we were both competing for different components of Hal's attention and, if that were the case, I could not think of a better sparring partner than Timothy. I didn't believe a word about his past. I didn't believe anything he said. I respected him.

He loosened his grip. "I'll make you a drink," he said, with a false gentlemanly air.

"Thank you, that would be lovely." I feigned a ladylike comeback.

Our conversation changed to accommodate our newfound tolerance for each other. We would be like dancing partners on board Hal's yacht, and Hal would be unaware of the music playing. Timothy was a brooding man in his late thirties, whose face was wrinkled not from laugh lines, but from stress. It was possible, as Hal believed, that he had worked very hard to achieve financial success, but it was also likely that he had used his obvious guile.

Timothy sat back on the open deck, reaching into the ice bucket, and filled two hi-ball glasses. He rummaged through the liquor cabinet like a professional, selecting nothing but the finest on someone else's account.

"You've found a good provider in Hal," he observed.

I wanted to tell him that he had, as well, but to be so blunt would only upset the balance.

"In contrast to what you might believe, Mr Dappler, Hal and I are very much in love."

Timothy laughed.

"Do you love your wife, Timothy?"

He looked at me with disgust. How could I have asked? he seemed to be wondering. "Love is complicated, Julie, and when you've been married as long as I have, marriage becomes complicated, too."

"I didn't think so," I said.

"What makes you so sure you're in love with Hal?"

"What makes you so interested in my feelings?"

He handed one of the two glasses to me. As I took mine, he raised his and we clinked. He nodded. "You're a smart woman, Julie—smarter than Hal knows."

"I'd say 'thank you', but I'm not convinced you're giving me a compliment."

"I am."

"Thank you, then."

We sat in silence for a while. Not an awkward silence, but a deliberate one. The sun was blinding and, for the first time, I managed to enjoy my very first sailing experience. Regardless of company, I was here and I was capable of making a life for myself amidst characters like Timothy who, years before, might have frightened me with their forthright statements.

"Just so you know, Timothy, I have no intention of becoming the kind of wife you so obviously loathe."

"What?" He snapped into attention. Maybe I had interrupted a daydream.

"I mean that Hal and I can both do what we choose. Hal is an attractive man and I'm only one flavour in a giant smorgasbord. I don't believe it's fair to force him to limit himself to me."

"But you're beautiful and charming. I think he'd be hard-pressed to find any woman more wonderful."

"That still doesn't mean that he should limit himself to me." I winked. "After all, there are some things that a lady cannot provide. Am I right?" I sipped my bourbon.

"I'm not trying to seduce Hal's pocketbook, as you're implying," Timothy protested.

He coughed. He was uncomfortable, and that was how I knew that I had struck a chord of truth with him. Had he thought about it, he would have realised that I had implied no such thing. There was an awkward silence, as is bound to happen when subtlety turns to practicality and gentility is laid to rest for a while.

"Timothy, I'll be honest with you. You are a charming and attractive man. You're handsome and a real gentleman."

"Thank you." He was hanging sceptically on to my words, as though I were a fortune teller about to reveal a truth he had never been able to access.

"Let me be more blunt. Hal and I have yet to consummate our love for one another."

"And why is that, Julie?"

"Why do you think?" I whispered.

"Um..."

"Exactly."

* * * *

Hal woke up from his nap and joined us above on the deck.

"Good evening, darling." I embraced him and kissed his cheek.

"Hello, you two." He smiled, still sleepy. "Timothy, I trust you've taken good care of my lady while I was downstairs. It's nice to see the two of you getting acquainted."

"Oh, we've been enjoying each other's company, Hal, don't you worry about us. Come have a drink," I ordered.

Sam, our cook, brought out a quiche and salad, and we opened a bottle of wine and enjoyed the gentle rocking motion of the boat. The warmth of the evening sun made both of their faces bright and glowing.

"You look lovely in this light, Julie, if you don't mind my saying," said Timothy.

"Why, thank you. As do the both of you."

I got up from my seat and planted myself on Hal's lap. He looked overwhelmed and slightly afraid, just as he would have had we been in private. It was nine o'clock and our captain, first mate and the cook had retired for the evening. It was just the three of us and it was getting dark. Timothy lit the lanterns and filled our drinks. I tucked my head into Hal's neck for a brief moment.

"Would you two like to be alone?" Timothy asked.

"Absolutely not," I said. "Tell him, darling."

"Stay. Stay, Timothy," Hal said, and it warmed my heart in a way I could not have foreseen. I really was thrilled to watch this adventure unfold. Although I had thought that I might only be interested in Hal's money, I now understood that I was much more interested in him — I was fascinated by this project, not because of the personal gain, but precisely the opposite. I was about to do both of these men the kind of favour that is never done. I was holding up mirrors.

I kissed Hal's cheek. Timothy tried to make light of the awkwardness with small talk. Hal followed suit. These two would do anything to avoid what was right in front of them. Like a curious kitten, I persisted. I cupped Hal's crotch with my hand and gave a gentle squeeze, then I stroked his inner thigh. Hal had failed to achieve hardness at all when we were alone. But that night, with Hal watching Timothy and Timothy watching us, I felt a tingle. I could feel Hal's excitement underneath the khaki cloth of his sailing pants. His white-collared shirt hung loosely untucked and I swivelled around, turned my back to Hal and faced Timothy instead.

"Timothy, you're a lovely, lovely man," I said. "Wouldn't you agree, Hal? Don't you think Timothy looks fantastic in this light?"

I turned back to Hal and saw he was nodding.

"It's a shame your wife isn't here, Timothy. I'm sure she would love to see you like this. We can tell her all about it, but it's just not going to be the same. I'm sure if she were here she'd want to do exactly what I'd like to do."

"What's that, darling?" Hal asked.

"Kiss Timothy. Isn't he a perfectly kissable gentleman? Don't you also want to kiss Timothy?"

Hal cleared his throat. I felt him throbbing beneath me. Timothy was speechless. It was almost effortless, having these two confront each other and come face to face. All I had to do was be between them.

"Hal? Would you mind if I kissed Timothy?"

"No, darling, I think that should be just fine."

"Timothy, would you mind if I kiss you?"

He shook his head, moved in towards my face with open lips. He was soft and warm and I could taste the bourbon on his breath. I could tell that he'd wanted me from the start. Our different agendas had nothing to do with our attraction for each other. He really was a fine collaborator. The dance was lovely.

I pushed myself firmly against Hal's bulging crotch as I wrapped my hands around Timothy's neck and pulled him in closer. He was leaning over, accommodating my sitting position, so I reached to the side and pulled a stool from beneath the table for him to sit on. Then I took his hands, cupped his palms and guided them to my breasts. He fondled me firmly as our tongues intertwined.

Poor Hal started sweating underneath us. I couldn't decide if it was the weight of us, the heat we produced or the thought that his wildest fantasy was mere minutes away.

Timothy found my nipples and squeezed. The rush, the sensation, pulsated through me. I love the feeling my nipples give me. I become hungry and needy and I obsess about surrendering to what they want and what they need. Men, it is said, live for their cocks. If that is true, I know the feeling and I know that I have it worse than men. My nipples wanted nothing more than for Timothy to rip my clothes off and fuck me right in front of Hal. My mind and body would follow their lead.

I moaned with such pleasure at Timothy's touch that the two men each let out moans despite their uneasiness. Discomfort had no place among us anymore, and to prove it to them, I separated from Timothy's lips long enough to say, "Now, gentlemen, before this goes any further, I need just one thing from each of you."

"What's that?"

"Anything."

"What happens at sea stays at sea. I'm a lady and you wouldn't want to sully my reputation, would you?"

They shook their heads. For a brief moment I was headmistress of my own private boys' school and they were my pupils of choice. "One more thing. I want you to kiss."

"What?" Timothy was in disbelief.

"Kiss," I restated.

Hal looked baffled for a moment, as if I had single-handedly humiliated him. Perhaps I shouldn't have said anything. Maybe I should have just let it happen. But I was a woman of intent. I had a plan and they needed to know that it was *my* plan they were following. This wasn't just a random occurrence but a well-choreographed event. Still puzzled, they looked at each other and at me. It was as though they needed my permission. It was as though I was a lady and incapable of ingesting the sight. In fact, I could think of no greater turn-on.

"I mean it, boys. Now." I stroked their cheeks. I was still seated on Hal's lap when Timothy leaned in past me and gently kissed him. The sight of my two companions, so rugged and manly compared to me, being delicate with each other, with their eyes closed and their lips relaxed, was more than I could stand. I felt as if I had already seen so much. Kelly had taught me that men would do anything for an attractive woman. When she and I had kissed, I'd loved it more than whatever audience we were trying to please. This was different. Without my even taking part in the physical sensations, just being privy to their arousal held such intricate power and grace for me.

Beneath me, I felt Hal swell to a magnitude I would not have imagined. The poor gentleman had spent decades depriving himself of that which his body craved. It was possible that he took his satisfaction from some secret source, but I was doubtful of it. It seemed as though he had not confronted the years and years of etiquette and backwards upbringing. He, like so many people, felt ashamed of his desires and had therefore never involved anyone in them, which was entirely unfortunate.

My vantage point was spectacular. The growing bulge below me was only upstaged by the gigantic package in front of me. I stroked Timothy's cock through his pants as he sat across from me kissing Hal and, intermittently, kissing me. I turned and kissed Hal too but, to my devastation, this decreased my very padded seat and so I decided against doing it again.

I knew that, in order for Hal to be happy, I would have to excuse myself fairly soon. But in order to be fair to myself, which was always my first priority, I needed a little attention from Timothy. I unzipped his pants, the sound of which made Hal tense up with delight. I inserted my hand and felt Timothy's massive cock as it threatened to spring from inside. I unbuttoned the top of his pants and he eagerly continued the process, pulling them off entirely along with his boxers.

In front of Hal and I stood the most impressive sight imaginable. We must have looked like shocked theatre-goers at the marvel of Timothy's beautiful erection. I was the first to take it into my mouth but I had no trouble sharing. Inside my mouth, Timothy felt even bigger than he looked. His face glistened with the kind of anticipation only brought on by the knowledge of orgasmic pleasure. I wondered what was going through his mind. Would he prefer to come in my mouth? In Hal's? In my cunt? In Hal's ass? On our faces? There was no way of knowing and so I let the idea pass through me, thinking instead about what I wanted. Right now what I wanted was to be utterly filled by Timothy's hard cock, but I would have to show a tiny bit of restraint and wait my turn.

Watching Hal engulf Timothy's cock with his lips was almost as good as doing it myself. He made the most amazing almost gagging sounds as he took the cock in towards the back of his throat.

"You're a good boy, Hal. You're such a good boy," I said as I rubbed his willing cock. He was much better about this than he had been about my kissing him. It probably wouldn't matter what I did to him — with a cock that size down his throat, he was completely distracted. Timothy closed his eyes and leant backwards, stretching like an acrobat. He looked Romanesque, a bit god-like, with the severity of his features all collaborating to please himself.

I could feel my own wetness take over my patience with these two. I unzipped Hal's pants and undid his button and he promptly removed his mouth from Timothy's cock long enough for me to take control of the situation again. Timothy unbuttoned my shirt, exposing my nipples and leant down to take one in his mouth. Hal, who had paused only to disrobe, moved back towards Timothy's cock.

"Not so fast, Hal. You must learn to share," I interrupted. He looked stunned. "You're the Southerner. You fellows invented the rule. Ladies first."

As a gesture of kindness I took his hand and guided it to his bulge, suggestively placing it so that he could stroke himself, which he did. I seated Timothy on the stool again and faced Hal as I carefully placed myself atop Timothy's solid cock. Timothy, gentle as he had been with Hal, seemed eager to feel himself inside me. He grabbed my hips and plunged me down on top of him as he let out a massive sigh. I moaned too and loved the feeling of my cunt stretching to accommodate him. I also loved having Hal there. "I want you to be able to see my face when I come, Hal," I whispered to him. "I want that for both of us."

It might have been the wrong thing to say, but I didn't care. I was in the presence of two highly aroused men and, whether or not I really was the centre of attraction, I was in my own experience. I thrust myself harder and harder onto Timothy's pulsating cock. His moans drove me towards the edge, as did his firm grasp on my hips. I guided his forefinger to my desperate clit. He knew just how to touch me. At his light tapping motion on my clitoris and hard thrusting deep inside me, I let out a howl unencumbered by anything, even the awareness that the crew was within earshot. We were at sea and this knowledge freed me to pant and moan and scream as I wished. The ocean unleashed me. I squeezed my own nipples as I came, grasping Timothy's massive erection with my muscles.

As inconsiderate as most men, Timothy kept pumping into me during and after my orgasm. I motioned for him to stop, then kissed them both graciously as I climbed off Timothy's cock. He grabbed my hair and brought me to my knees with ease. I was in front of him in seconds, my clitoris still wildly throbbing. I took his hardness into my mouth and tasted my own juices on him. I was utterly satisfied and, despite that this was not a relay race, I wanted to pass the baton along to another eager participant.

I substituted my hand for my mouth. Stroking Timothy, I stood up, kissed him goodnight on the lips and Hal on the cheek. With one hand on Timothy, I grabbed Hal's hair with the other, forcing him into my previous position. When I left them, Hal was on his knees, Timothy's cock buried deep inside his mouth.

"Goodnight, boys." I walked off.

In response, I heard some muffled versions of niceties. I was only steps away when their moans turned louder.

The next morning, I was up long before the two of them. Hal had not come to join me in our double bed. If this was what lay ahead, I thought, as I peeked over the covers in my beautiful, comfortable and gigantic bed, then the future would be sweet.

Chapter Seven

For days, Hal and Timothy and I found permutations of that first night together. We hardly slept at all. I would wake up to their sounds and lay in bed stroking my nipples and caressing my pussy as I imagined the actions that went along with the sounds. Being at sea with them, in that tiny vessel, was marvellous. It could have been terrible. It almost had been. When, at first, I hadn't understood Timothy's motivation and he hadn't understood mine, I'd been certain it would be a long trip to Florida.

But Timothy and I, once we understood that we were somehow accomplices in the sacred world of secrets, enjoyed each other immensely. I tried to be as generous towards the two men as I could, allowing them their time and space without my presence. I was sure that Hal noticed. I could sense that this facet of my behaviour separated me from any previous women in his life. Still, there were times when I just needed to feel the presence of a body flush against my skin.

Perhaps it was this appetite for skin that led me to befriend Sam. In addition to titillating my taste buds with her excellent meals, she was also strong and sturdy and had noticed me immediately. It was mutual. I saw her when Hal held his outstretched hand for me to board at the dock. She was in the back, preparing drinks for us, one eyebrow raised at me. She, too, had figured out Hal's preferences, I was sure, because she had looked surprised to see me there. Perhaps she had been hoping to occupy my space in Hal's life, to win him over and claim the sweet life for herself, but somehow I didn't think so.

Sam was a lovely woman, I thought. She wasn't feminine, nor was she polite. I admired her. I had never met anyone like her before, which was partly why she'd caught my eye and also how she had managed to develop such a grasp on me. She seemed to live in her own world as she laboured on board the ship. For the first two nights, she didn't even speak to me. I wasn't a fan of small talk myself, so I simply upheld the code she lived by.

Hal told me she had been on board his boat for years. He hired his captains on a contract basis, but Sam lived on the boat full-time. When we docked in Florida, she would sail it to wherever Hal kept it moored and go back to her private life. It was an arrangement that suited them both. Picturing her living on board the yacht all year round, with only her own company, gave her the mystique of a cabin-dwelling woodsman. I had to get to know her better, despite my fear that the divide between us was too great to overcome.

On the third morning, I called her in from my bed.

"Could I have some coffee and a croissant?" I asked in my most cheerful morning voice.

This only aroused agitation in Sam, who rolled her eyes as she turned towards the door. She hated taking orders, that much was obvious.

With a vaguely polite nod, she returned with my breakfast and placed it neatly at the table by my bed.

"There you are, miss," she said, rather mockingly. I knew she thought I was lazy and that I should have got out of bed. I could tell she'd cursed me, the way she probably cursed most Southern ladies, these airs of importance not registering on her measuring scale.

"Julie."

"Hmm?" She wasn't interested. She probably believed that after we reached Florida she would never see me again.

"Call me Julie," I insisted.

"Okay, Julie. Can I get you anything else?" she asked.

"Not right now. Sit down." I put my hand out and gestured to the side of my bed.

"I have work to do."

"It can wait," I smiled. "Can't it?"

"How would you know?"

"Mmm. Good point. I wouldn't," I sipped my coffee. "This is delicious. Thank you."

"What, are you lonely or something?" she asked.

"No."

"Then why talk to me? Don't you have gentlemen to entertain?" Her tone was gruff. She did not seem easily impressed in general, and she was not impressed with me at all.

"They're taking care of each other. They can wait."

"I'm sure they can. I can't say the same about lunch, but you wouldn't know about that, either. Lunch just sort of happens in your world, doesn't it?"

"Sam. Relax. They can wait. So can lunch. Sit down."

She sat on my bed, leaning on her strong arms. I've always had a weakness for the uninterested. It makes me want to win their favour, as a matter of principle. It brings out my determination. So much for courting for money. I also court for sport.

Sam buffed her fingernails on her jeans as though she was waiting for me to say something or do something. It was as though, without the contract of her job and my position as Hal's guest, the two of us had nothing in common and nothing to talk about. I decided that the best thing to do was to launch into this directly, the way one cuts open a piece of meat in the oven to test whether it's done.

"Sam, I find you very attractive." I tried my seductive voice and a smile as I blew the steam from my coffee cup.

"Attractive?" She was either caught off guard or else repulsed.

"Good looking," I reiterated.

She looked a little puzzled. She either hadn't expected me to say such a thing, or else hadn't wanted me to. "I'm in a relationship," she said, matter-of-factly. "I'm taken."

"Well how does that change anything?" I asked. "Can't I still find you attractive?"

"I suppose you could. You probably find everyone attractive."

This was strange, an odd betrayal of what I thought of as our new bond. "What do you mean?"

"You know. You. Timothy. You. Hal."

"A girl has needs."

"For what? Diamonds?"

Her bluntness was so pedestrian. Didn't she get it? I had worked hard. I had earned all of this. I was open-minded and non-judgemental and, because of it, I had landed myself an excellent opportunity to acquire a fortune, and here she was trying to make me feel guilty about it. I didn't even know how to respond.

"You really think I'm just here for the money?"

"Yep." She was so calm about it. She had assessed me and thought she had figured out everything there was to know about me.

"Well, you're wrong." It wasn't the best comeback line. I wasn't proud of myself, but what could I say? I hadn't encountered someone like her before. Timothy had been on to me, but only out of some kind of competition. Timothy had been careful about his words — he had tried to deliver mixed messages and gauge my responses. Sam outright didn't care. She didn't care if she hurt my feelings or if she made me uncomfortable. She probably didn't even care that, if I wanted to, I could have her fired. And her indifference to that fact turned me on incredibly.

"Look, no offence, you're probably a nice girl or whatever but I've known Hal for years. I know, okay. Hell, I'd marry him myself to help him out, he's a good guy. But the authorities probably wouldn't buy it, you know?"

"He is a good guy. I love him," I said, startled by how ignorant it sounded.

"Whatever. I have to go, Julie," she said as she got up to leave, patting down her white chef's shirt.

"Please stay. I wanted to... I don't know...get to know you more."

"I don't have time," she said, and slipped out of my room.

That was *my* strategy. That was *my* game. How strange it was to see it reflected back at me and to see how well it worked. Her rugged presence left its mark on my morning and an impact on me that I could not shake. Being ignored really was hot.

I spent the morning alone in bed until Hal came and joined me. He was flushed when he came into the room. I was sitting up, still in my camisole, with my empty plate and cup beside me. I lifted the covers and he crawled into bed with me, limp as a tired puppy, and fell asleep. I curled up beside him and we napped together, my arm lazily draped around him.

By mid afternoon, we'd started to wake up. He looked at me, smiled, and said, "You're amazing."

"Why?" I asked.

"Well, not very many women would be as understanding as you are."

"You're a gem, Hal. There isn't that much to understand."

"I want to make you happy. I promise I'll make you happy."

"I already am happy, Hal. Don't you see that?"

"I mean really happy." He got up, fumbled around his luggage and underneath a pile of his strewn clothes. "I have something for you."

I sat up. My hair was a mess. I was tired from napping all day. It was strange to lose track of the day like this, but time was irrelevant on board the boat. Outside, it was nice to pay attention to the weather but from the comfort of my luxurious bed I could hide from the world in a way that pleased me.

"Hal," I whispered and stretched my hand out to him. He came back to bed, taking my hand and sitting down on the edge of the mattress. "I meant what I said the other night. That thing about you being a good boy. You are. You're a good man."

He cupped my face in his hands. "That's not true. If I was such a good man, I would have been able to..."

His eyes pierced through me. It seemed crazy, since we barely knew each other. We each had our calculating motivations for being there, but I thought for an instant that I loved him. At least, I felt for him what I had never felt for any man, which was a type of camaraderie. It was different from the obsession I'd had with Kelly. Kelly and I had watched our own backs. We could leave each other and not regret it. We were similar creatures that way. Hal felt more like a child, not in a bad way but in a kind of sensitive way. He brought out a new feeling in me. I wanted to protect him and cradle him at the same time as I wanted to see him do what was right for him. It was almost impossible to express this to him.

"I want to be with you, Hal. I don't need us to be together in that way. You have to believe me."

"I'm not letting you down?"

"No."

"Is it because you're not attracted to me?"

"Darling! You're wonderful. I want to be with you because you're wonderful. You make me happy, and I think the world of you, and it gives me a lot of joy to see you enjoy Timothy's company as well."

"Really? How can it?"

"It's hard to explain. I'm not the jealous type. I'm not interested in tying you down. I'm interested in setting you free."

I meant it. Everyone inevitably ties someone down or is tied down by someone else. All my life, I'd seen it everywhere. My parents were like that. Everyone's parents are like that. All my clients with wives came to me not for sex, but for a glimmer of hope that they had some remnant of freedom left. I was not interested in taking Hal's freedom, nor could I ever be interested in giving mine to him. I think it was this realisation that freed my heart to love him sincerely.

He didn't know what to say, and so he simply looked down at his hands.

"Love is many things. Love doesn't have to mean that we share a bed. Though I like sharing a bed with you. We can sleep together and you can fuck other people. I can fuck other people and we can still love each other," I told him.

"Do you love me?"

"I do, Hal. I love you." The words had never left my mouth before, and I was surprised at how easily they'd flowed out of me. I had always thought the statement so trite. It was the kind of thing that bored people say out of obligation. That's what I had thought until I'd felt it.

"I love you too, Julie," he said back, and I leaned towards him, grabbed his big head between my hands and kissed his forehead.

"See?"

"What?"

"Love is many things," I said. "I know I'm different from other women. Believe me. I know."

"You most certainly are. I would never want to change that."

"Come on. Let's get dressed and go out onto the deck for a while. I'm going to see if I can charm Sam."

"Sam? Why would you charm Sam?" He was baffled.

"Because she needs it." I smiled and reached for my hairbrush.

"What did you do before I met you, Miss Julie? Were you really a journalist like you said you were?"

"I kept a journal." I laughed.

"Well, I don't care where you came from or what you did, I'll have you know. I love you. I want you to stay with me forever. You don't ever have to leave my side."

"Timothy's welcome, too, you know."

"Ah, Timothy, that rascal. He'll be gone as soon as we dock in Florida. He's a man on the move. I've known Timothy for years — know him a bit better now, I would say — but he's not the staying type. Anyway, his wife wouldn't like that much."

"I'm glad you're enjoying each other's company. It pleases me to see you with your friends." We exchanged knowing glances.

"And it pleases me to see you with my friends, too."

"Oh, stop!" I slapped his arm. "You're embarrassing me."

"No, really. I mean it. If you want a little time with Timothy, I'll make room for that. I understand it."

"Tonight, I'm more interested in Sam."

"So you say. I can't say I understand it. She's not much of a lady."

"Neither am I." I winked.

He was dressed and out of the room before I even left the warmth of my bed.

Chapter Eight

Sam seemed the kind of woman who would be put off by dresses and fancy outfits. She would not be interested in accessories or frills. She was a pragmatist, and so I decided to wear plain jeans, a simple, white turtleneck sweater and my hair in a ponytail. She had won the first round, but I had a plan. I've always prided myself on being an excellent judge of character. I was not sure what I wanted to transpire between us, but I was determined to get a reaction from her. I was very demanding of everyone's attention — I needed the rush of knowing that everyone in the room wanted me. She had held out on me — determined, perhaps, to stay faithful to whomever was waiting for her on land. But things, it seems, are different at sea. Things happen on the water that become legend, quite literally detached from anything else.

After a quick drink with the boys on the deck, I slipped into the kitchen quite casually, even though there was nothing casual about it.

"So, tell me about her," I said to Sam, who was busily chopping vegetables.

"Who?"

"Your lover."

"How do you know my lover is a woman?"

"Because I make you uncomfortable."

"I'm not uncomfortable. I just don't like you."

"You don't know me."

"I know your type. You're not the first woman Hal has brought on board."

"I'll be the last, though."

She stopped what she was doing, looked at me for a moment and shook her head. "So full of yourself."

"I'm not saying it to be full of myself. I'm merely stating fact. But enough about me. Let's talk about things you like. How long have you worked for Hal?"

"Since he bought the yacht. I've been on the yacht for the last two owners. She's a beauty. That's why she changes hands so often. I'm sure you're familiar with the concept."

She seemed pleased with herself every time she made a backhanded remark. It didn't matter. There was something about her. Her level of comfort and security. Nothing fazed her. She didn't care about the consequences of speaking her mind. God, I loved that.

"Yep. She's been bought and sold by British corporals, an Australian tycoon...and now Mr Confederation himself." She had such disdain for everyone. I flinched at her gruffness.

"But you've stayed loyal to the ship. Why?"

"Why not? Like I said, she's a beauty. Look at the railings. She was built in the twenties. They don't even make the kind of finishings that she's equipped with anymore. We've been around the world together three times over. Hal doesn't like to go far, but boy—that Australian, he sure did."

"What do you do the rest of the time?"

"What do you mean?"

"On land."

"As little as possible. Haven't had a land job for decades."

"So this yacht is the lady you're saving yourself for, then?"

She smiled. Her eyes were warm with confusion. How had I figured out her conundrum? she seemed to be wondering. How did I know anything about her at all? I loved to prove people wrong when they expected so little of me. How quickly her tone changed. She pointed her knife at me, bobbing it up and down. She'd been had, all right. And she had nothing to say for herself.

"Join me on the deck for a drink," I commanded.

"I can't. I'm working."

"You're going to work yourself to death. Learn to live a little," I insisted.

She continued chopping, not even remotely considering my invitation. "This is how Hal wants it."

"Hal this, Hal that. I thought you had a mind of your own."

"I also have a job that I love."

"Well, Hal's busy anyway. Besides, I'm pleading with you." I smiled. "And I'm relentless."

"Fine. Then you have to come back with me and help me."

"What?"

"You heard me, woman." She was pleased with herself at this phrase.

"You're on." I reached my outstretched hand towards hers and we shook on the deal.

"For the rest of the trip," she said, still shaking my hand.

I nodded. I didn't know what else to do.

Outside, on the deck, Sam's skin had a healthy glow. I hadn't noticed inside but in the sun her boyish face was ageing nicely. She had just a few smile lines around her eyes and one that went across the bridge of her nose. All seemed like indications of fascinating experiences.

She only stayed on the deck with me for the duration of the obligatory drink. Then she excused herself to finish taking inventory and make up a list of groceries for the rest of the trip.

It was mid afternoon when we pulled into the harbour at Duke's Point for refuelling and refreshing of supplies. That night and early the following morning, I savoured every moment before I had to get to work at Sam's job. I stayed alone on board the yacht, unsure why everyone else was so eager to get off. I wanted a glimpse of Sam's introverted life.

Timothy and Hal took a walk into the city. Sam and the captain and his first mate went off in separate directions. I retired to my bedroom, determined to convince Sam to fuck me before Florida. It had started as a matter of principle but it had become a matter of great need. How could she go on like this? Was she as cruel and uninterested as she let on? Then why was she so much fun?

Timothy's face was pale when he and Hal returned with lobsters for tonight's dinner. They had been to town, where Timothy had found a payphone and called his wife.

"She's meeting us at the harbour in Florida," he announced.

"Great," I said, "the more the merrier." I had been hoping, for Timothy's wife's sake, that she was an imaginary figure—a story, just like the ones he told about his hard work in New York City. He only ever spoke of her as a nag and a horribly controlling woman. But speaking of spouses when they aren't present, especially in like-minded company, can often lead to less than complimentary descriptions. How did I figure in Hal's discussions when we were apart? It didn't much matter to me, as long as we enjoyed each other when we were able to be together.

"She's not like us." He looked concerned.

"No one is like us," Hal said. "We're quite the motley collection." And his warm laughter melted my heart. I felt as though I belonged here. I had experienced friendship so few times, and I have come to believe that true friendship exists in magical moments, cut off from long-term commitments. I was able to put aside my scepticism while we were sailing because there were so many better things to do. There is no point in being doubtful of other people's motivations when you're at sea. It's more like a primal need to get along laced with the eternal will to survive.

Hal and I clinked our glasses in the afternoon sun. "Do you know her?" I asked.

"Haven't met her. I hear she's quite the lady," Hal said. And as he said it, it occurred to me that 'lady' could be a derogatory term.

I had been aspiring to become one even though I knew, deep down, that I could never attain that kind of stature. I could fake it but, on some level, a lady is born rather than made. Maybe it didn't matter. When men spoke of ladies, they would say the word in a way that suggested something else. I had a feeling that Timothy's wife was a monster.

"What does that mean, 'she's quite the lady'?" I asked them both.

"It means she's nothing like you," Timothy said, point blank.

"But what does that mean?"

"It means we like you." Hal laughed.

"You don't like your wife?" I looked at Timothy. "What are you with her for, then?"

"It's complicated." He sipped his martini.

"In other words, it's for the cash," I whispered as Hal turned to reach for the ice bucket.

Timothy said nothing to my statement. He looked down as though he was thinking about it for a brief second, then he shook it from his conscience altogether, smiled at me and clinked my glass. "To the greatest lady I've ever known." He raised his martini high in the air and Hal, who hadn't been paying attention until just then, turned to me and said, "Here, here. The greatest lady ever."

It seemed somehow strange that they were so adamant in their accolades for me. I had never quite felt as if I'd belonged with anyone before, but maybe the reason was quite simply that I hadn't. I'd never had girlfriends growing up. They hadn't interested me — they'd seemed so silly and uptight. I felt as if Hal and Timothy had become excellent friends.

"Well, boys, I have to go. Sam needs me in the kitchen."

"You're working?" Hal was shocked.

"Serving, actually. Serving her. I'm doing whatever she wants me to do."

"Why?" Timothy asked.

"It's complicated." I laughed. "And she's hot. What's a girl to do?" I strutted out of the cabin and left them staring, shaking their heads, confused by something I knew they could not see.

In the kitchen, Sam had her head in the fridge. I didn't think she'd heard me come in, but she mumbled, "You're late." Then she looked at me. "What are you wearing?"

I eyed my white turtleneck and jeans and shrugged.

"This is kitchen work, sweetie." She was so firm. "Get changed."

"But this is the most casual outfit I have." It was true. When Hal had bought me a wardrobe before we'd left, I hadn't thought I would need work slacks. I'd only bought dresses and this pair of designer jeans.

"It figures." She rolled her eyes in my direction. "You can't wear your fancy clothes in my kitchen. Take them off and put this on instead." She tossed a white bundle to me. I caught it mid-air.

I looked at the fabric. It was just an apron. Two could definitely play at this game. I undressed, neatly folded and placed my clothes in a pile underneath the counter. The apron could not possibly cover my erect nipples. I was sure Sam had planned it that way. I was incredibly turned on at the idea that she might take me right there in the kitchen.

"I need these mushrooms cleaned and washed," she said, handing me a big, stainless steel bowl.

"Are you serious?" I was disbelieving. Hadn't she just asked me to get undressed? Had I missed something?

"Get to work," she barked.

Fine, I thought. *Suit yourself.*

But she *was* suiting herself. This was exactly what she wanted — to drive me crazy with desire and to then further pretend that she did not care at all. It was so strange. I stood there, naked, rinsing mushrooms in her sink with a tiny, gentle-bristled brush. She wasn't even looking at me from her side of the kitchen, where she was busy with various containers. If I hadn't been naked and aroused, I would have felt as if I were working in the kitchen with my mother, or working as a prep cook in some dodgy restaurant somewhere with a very stern manager. This was not the kind of fun I had been expecting. It was more than fun. It was strange. Like meeting someone more adept at playing the part of me than I was.

"I'm finished," I said, once I had inspected all the mushrooms and carefully placed them in a new bowl.

"We'll see about that." She came up behind me. The heat that radiated off her body was more than I could handle. I wanted to melt back into her and feel my skin against hers. I could feel her breath on my neck as she leaned over me. She was quite a bit larger than me, a really staunch-looking, capable woman. She, predictably, did not seem fazed at all by our closeness. She was, after all, wearing pants. It was me who was the more susceptible of the two of us.

"This won't do," she said. "Look, here — what's this?" She picked one of the white mushrooms out of the bowl and held it close to my face. "See?"

I shook my head.

"Dirt."

"Where?"

"Don't pretend you don't see it. You were negligent and you know it. And you know what happens to negligent kitchen girls..."

"No." It was true. I didn't.

"They get punished. They have to do the same chore over again." She looked me in the eye. Had it been anyone but her, I would have assumed they were joking, but Sam didn't look amused. "You heard me. Get to work." She put the bowl down so hard that some of the mushrooms ricocheted off the side and spilled into the sink.

"Yes, ma'am," I said.

"What was that you said?"

"Yes, ma'am," I repeated, and gulped.

"Yes, *sir*," she said.

"Yes, sir," I repeated.

"And you can think about that while you clean this next round."

"I will, sir."

My hands were wrinkled and pruny by the time I called her back over, and she still managed to find a tiny speck of dirt, even though I had spent almost an hour ensuring each mushroom's utter perfection. She was unbelievable.

Then she assigned a most putrid task. She ordered me to scrub the floors on my hands and knees.

"You do realise I'm not wearing anything," I pointed out, trying to appeal to her sympathy, which I learned was futile wishful thinking on my part.

"I guess it'll be easier for you to clean yourself up afterwards," she said.

Some sympathetic character she was. *My perfectly exfoliated, perfectly waxed, perfectly moisturised legs on this filthy floor?* I almost refused. But this was a meeting of minds and if anyone was determined, it was me. There was no way I would back out on anything, no matter how far she pushed me. How far could she possibly push me?

I started by sweeping. Then I got down with a bucket of hot, soapy water, a hard brush and a thick rag, and began. My nails felt as if they were going to peel right off my fingers. The soap stung my skin and my knees went immediately red. All I could think about was her approval. I tried to guess what she would disapprove of next. She was impossible to please.

It took me two hours but I scrubbed the filthy floor to perfection. I almost thought she had forgotten about me, because she left without saying a word. I had been tempted to stop when I'd finished the initial scrub, but I'd known better than to walk away before she'd had a chance to come and inspect my work.

By the time she came back, I was ready to burst into tears. I had worked so hard. I was sweaty and felt awful and she had pushed me so far. My hair was a mess, I had dirt under my nails and my knees were scraped. I had even slipped on the floor and had a bruise on my hip from the fall.

"I'm finished, sir," I said when she came back.

"Are you sure about that?" She smiled. She wasn't bothered at all that I had slaved away for her all afternoon.

"I'm fairly certain, sir."

"Not entirely certain?"

"Well, no, sir. Not until you inspect my work, sir." My face was flushed. I was so tired, I felt like fainting.

"Good girl," Sam stated as a matter of fact.

They were the first nice words she'd said to me since we'd met.

I beamed. I could feel myself blushing. I could feel the rush of her attention on me. Things would change now, I was sure. Oh, yes, she was coming to see what a great servant I could be, and I had earned her respect with my diligence.

"Now, get to work on the bathroom."

"What?"

"You heard me."

"I thought that..."

"You thought that what? This was some kind of game? That I don't really mean what I say? You think I'm giving you orders for you to ignore them? Is that what you think?"

"No, sir."

"That's better. Now, scrub that bathroom. I don't want a single speck in there. Every surface disinfected. You got that?"

"Yes, sir."

"Good."

With that, she left again. I wondered what I was doing there in my apron, naked and hurting. Had I not agreed to be Hal's lady? This was not what ladies did. So why was I here? Why couldn't I prise myself away from Sam's relentless task giving?

She came back only to dismiss me for the evening.

"Your job here is done. I'll see you tomorrow morning bright and early for the breakfast shift. Come dressed appropriately this time." Then she walked away. She didn't even look me up and down, just mumbled under her breath, "You're filthy. Clean yourself up."

Chapter Nine

Upstairs, I tried to avoid Hal and Timothy, but inevitably that kind of plan fails. Hal just happened to be in our room, getting dressed for drinks on the deck, and he saw me. I hadn't even bothered to put my jeans back on. I just walked up with my dirty apron barely covering anything.

"What happened to you?" He chuckled.

"Sam. That's what."

He started laughing. I thought it was unfair.

"She's quite the stern one," he said.

I wasn't sure how he'd intuited that I was dirty from cleaning and not from having dirty sex all over the kitchen with Sam. Somehow that seemed unfair, too. Was I that transparent?

"Stern, yeah, that's an understatement," I said as I picked up my silk robe and walked into the bathroom to shower.

Upstairs, it became obvious that Hal had filled Timothy in on my day with Sam.

"So what'd she make you do?" Hal pestered. Timothy studied me intently.

"Never mind."

"Why'd you do it?"

"Look, you know nothing about it. You wouldn't understand. You wouldn't get it." I was tired, cranky and confused.

"Maybe not. But I would like my pillow fluffed. Would you be a doll and get that for me?" Timothy just couldn't help himself.

I rolled my eyes. "You're such an ass." I kicked his ankle under the table.

Then I remembered that I also had leverage. It wasn't the greatest feeling to have your friends at sea turn on you. There was nowhere to retreat to, nothing to do about it. Still, I couldn't help myself when it came to engaging in the other side of the equation.

"So, Timothy, when's your wife meeting us?" I asked casually as I stirred my drink.

Hal burst into his usual warm laughter.

It was dark. The deck was lit with lanterns and the shadows created such great effects on both of the men's faces. As I sipped away at my second drink, I felt, again, like the luckiest girl in the world to have friends like them. It was almost enough to distract me from my day's chores and the nagging, yet titillating, knowledge that the next morning would hold similar challenges.

The sexual frustration was killing me. If Sam wasn't going to fuck me at all, I was going to have to do something else. Maybe I'd have to fuck Timothy again, just to get the impulse off my chest. But I had come to appreciate what we had together. There was a special bond between us — the kind of bond that only a kindred spirit can have with her husband's lovers, which was when I realised that, indeed, I had started to think of Hal in that way. It had happened so naturally that I almost didn't understand it. My body had been so focused on Sam and, before her, Timothy, and before that, on the idea of Hal.

Timothy just smiled at my comment. It was a topic none of us wanted to entertain.

"This brings me to something," Hal announced. He straightened his collar, running his finger along the ridges as though it were too tight around the neck. Timothy and I looked at each other and turned to him. "All this talk of marriage..."

Timothy winked at me and touched my arm. My stomach was suddenly in knots. We had been to Duke's Point. I was busy plotting my seduction of Sam at the time. I hadn't been thinking. We had stopped, Hal had been to a city, the two fellows had been awfully sneaky since their return... I tried my best to be unassuming, but Hal fumbled through his pockets.

"Miss Julie?" He beamed. "Will you dance with me?"

He took my hand, Timothy turned up our CD player and we danced on the deck in the darkness of the summer night. It was perfect. I'd never thought about this kind of moment when I was growing up. I'm sure many girls did and, when they did, I'm sure they did not imagine that their suitor would be twice their age and uninterested in a sexual relationship with them, but this was my reality and I loved it. Timothy clapped and cheered and was wonderful as Hal pulled me closer, guided me back and forth across the deck. I laughed at how silly we must have looked, dancing there to an Eagles hit that I vaguely remembered from my dad's radio in the truck.

I leaned on Hal's chest, burying my giggles against his neck. The song stopped and I sat down.

"Timothy, you should join him. Dance. Come on," I urged.

Hal was dancing and gallivanting by himself. He was so sweet and secure in himself to be able to entertain us with his pantomime of a dance partner.

Hal took Timothy's hand and the two of them looked so lovely together. I smiled as I looked at them through the bottom of my glass. They were both fans of classic seventies tunes, it was obvious. They anticipated each beat and eloquently mouthed the words. Not even half a song went by before Timothy sat down again.

"Tonight's about you, Julie," he said.

"What about me?" I became very shy for the first time ever in front of them.

Hal just looked at me. He was smiling, shaking his head back and forth. "I never thought I would meet anyone like you, Julie. Come here." He took my hand again and pulled me from my chair.

I stood in front of him and he hugged me, then proceeded to crouch down on one knee.

"Oh my, Hal. Don't bother with that. You know I will," I said and took his hand and yanked him back to a standing position. I jumped up on him and wrapped my legs around his waist, steadying myself with my arms around his neck.

He put his arms around me. "You will? I'm so glad."

"That's the sweetest thing I've ever seen," Timothy said, and wiped a tear from his eye. "You two are the best. You really are, you know. The best. I mean it."

I couldn't help but cry a little as well, and suddenly we were all hugging, the three of us swaying back and forth in the warm summer air. It was perfect.

I did something that Hal probably wasn't expecting. I turned to him, with the two of them holding each other's hands around my back, and I kissed him. He kissed me back. It was really something. I had never had a best friend to kiss before. It wasn't the same between Kelly and me, but I imagined that this was what it felt like for any friends. It was a simple and dear expression, something we could do and then stop. It wasn't the kind of kiss that would lead to something tremendously arousing, but a kind of familiarising with the already familiar.

Then I turned from Hal and kissed Timothy, which made him tense up. It was the tension of arousal. My body reciprocated. My panties moistened immediately as I felt Timothy's hardness against my leg, and I savoured the sweet feeling of different kinds of love at the same time.

"Okay. Now you two," I ordered, and before the words had even left my mouth, they had locked lips with each other. It was so formidable how comfortable we were with each other.

We sat back down and Hal pulled the tiny box from his shirt pocket.

"It seems more appropriate if you put it on yourself," he said, as he slid it across the polished dark wood table. I took it in my palm and held it for a moment before opening the box. I had been expecting a diamond ring but, instead, he had bought me a massive ruby in a square shape.

"It's more royal," he explained. "I was thinking about it. Diamonds, to me, are for princesses. And you aren't that. I think of you more as a queen. Maybe not *my* queen, but a queen nonetheless..."

"Your own queen," Timothy added.

"Will you be my royal subjects?" I asked them.

"We'd have it no other way, m'lady," Timothy said.

I smiled at my ring. It really was regal looking. I had never thought about what kind of gemstone I was compatible with. It had not occurred to me to consider such things until recently and, even then, I think that kind of pondering is something one grows up with. I certainly hadn't. My mother's wedding ring had belonged to my dad's mother, and her mother before her. It had been a very convenient item exchanging hands for signification. That was all. It never would have occurred to my mother to question whether things could have been different. A gold band was a gold band, plain and simple.

I loved my ruby. I had always thought that jewellery was worth nothing more than its own net worth. I had been wrong. I was sure the ring had been expensive, but that was hardly the point. The point was that, to me, it had a value so much greater than its worth. It was representative. It meant that Hal and I honoured each other, trusted each other and would try to build a meaningful union together.

"It's beautiful, Hal. Absolutely stunning."

"Timothy helped pick it out," he said. He was always so humble about his gestures. He didn't seem to make a big deal about anything. He had really touched me. They both had.

"How perfect," I said. "Thank you both, then."

"I love it on you," Timothy said. "When's the big date?"

"I hadn't thought of that," I said. "I guess this means we're really doing it."

"Come to Virginia first. We'll have a formal courtship. You'll love it there. You can take it easy for the rest of the summer. We'll plan it for the fall," Hal said.

I excused myself early that evening. In my bed, I touched the ring on my finger. It felt as though the ring possessed magic powers. I turned it around, placing the ruby against my palm, and rubbed it with my thumb until I fell asleep.

* * * *

Early the next morning, I woke up, placed my ring in its box and left it under my pillow. I scurried to the kitchen. I wanted to be there before Sam to make a good impression with my punctuality.

Of course, she was already there, waiting for me.

"You just can't show up on time, can you?" was the first thing she asked as I walked through the door and saw her sipping her morning coffee. She was seated on the kitchen counter.

"I'm early."

"Not by my calculations."

"Sorry."

"I beg your pardon?"

"Sorry, sir."

She sipped at her coffee mug and watched me change into my uniform — again, naked underneath a newer, cleaner white apron. This time, I was less aroused, having lost faith in my ability to attract her.

"What would you like me to do this morning, sir?"

My question was met by a long, intense stare. I found it unnerving how she could make me feel as if I was in her way, when I had worked so hard to satisfy her.

"I've turned you into a good worker," she said. "In fact, you've become an excellent assistant."

"Thank you."

"And you know what happens to excellent assistants?" she asked.

"No."

"They are rewarded for their hard work."

With that, she got up from her seat and walked slowly and confidently towards me. "I love the way you look in that apron," she said.

"Thank you."

"And I loved watching you clean the mushrooms and scrub the floor yesterday."

"Thank you."

"Did you know I was watching you the whole time?"

"No."

"Well, I was," she whispered, mere centimetres from my ear.

"I'm glad I could please you, sir."

"Well, you haven't exactly pleased me yet, my kitchen tart."

"I haven't?" I pouted.

"No. But you will." She grabbed my hips in her firm grip and pulled me against her. My back was flush against her chest, just like the day before when she'd approached me from behind while I'd been cleaning the mushrooms. She moved her forefingers and thumbs slowly up my naked body to my awaiting nipples, and I felt simultaneous squeezes that sent shivers through me.

I moaned and leaned my head back into the nook between her neck and right shoulder. "How can I please you, sir? Anything."

She twirled me around. "When I first met you, I thought you were a high and mighty princess, but you're just a tart, aren't you?"

"For you? Yes." I didn't tell her that I was also Hal and Timothy's queen. That didn't matter.

She kissed me. It was firm and gentle, not like Kelly and not like Timothy or Hal. It was provocative and promising and made me want to melt into her. I was instantly weak, as if I needed to sit down. She must have sensed it, because she lifted me up onto the counter. It felt cold against my naked ass, and she seemed amused, watching me struggle to find comfort.

Sam's embrace was strong and deliberate. She held onto me with the kind of smoothness that made me trust her and want to surrender to her. She kissed my neck deeply and licked my collarbone, across my shoulders and finally took one of my nipples into her mouth, the way I had been fantasising about since the beginning. Her mouth felt so good against my flesh and the sensations from my nipples sent me into a frenzy. Wetness oozed out of me as I wrapped my legs around her waist and pulled her towards the counter. She, in turn, pulled me against her and started to rub her denim-covered crotch against my naked one. I was sure I would soak her jeans right through if we stayed like this for much longer, but we didn't.

She pushed me back against the counter and undid the knot of my apron behind my back. After a quick tug, the white fabric messily hung at my back and she had buried her face between my legs. She found my clitoris instantly with her tongue, and she moaned with glee.

"Your pussy is so sweet," she mumbled. Then, she returned to lapping at my desperate moisture.

I moaned and pulled her face closer and closer, wrapping my legs around her head. I neared orgasm quickly as she became more and more intent on stroking my clit with her tongue. She stopped quite suddenly, though, and pulled back. She stood up to meet my lips again. Tasting myself was another sweet reward.

She was panting and flushed and I was hot, my whole body twisting in desperate desire to feel more of her. She grabbed my hair with her left hand and held me in place as she kissed me, thrusting her tongue deep inside my mouth. With her right hand, she pushed her index finger inside me. Then she added her middle finger, opening my pussy up with her other hand, as if she owned me. The feeling of her fucking my pussy with her dextrous fingers was an immense turn-on. I was in heaven, completely oblivious to my surroundings, my travelling companions, anything. All I cared about was pleasing her, and she seemed pretty pleased with me.

I sat up and tried to unbutton her chef's shirt, but she pushed my hand away.

"Not yet," she said.

She shoved me back down onto the counter and, keeping her fingers deeply inserted inside me, she crouched down and licked my clit again, pressing firmly on me with her tongue. I couldn't hold back anymore. I started trembling and felt myself losing control. She held my legs in place over her shoulders as she pinned me down. She was in complete control the whole time. I would come when she wanted it — I knew that. I accepted it. And once I'd accepted it, it was easy.

She gently sucked at my clitoris, nibbling slightly at the sensitive skin, and thrust against me deep inside, in a way a cock never could. I felt an unfamiliar sensation come over me as her hand and mouth caused me to moan like I had never moaned before.

She was consistent and thorough, moving rhythmically as I approached climax.

That day I had so much more than a mere orgasm. In fact, that morning with Sam opened my eyes to a whole different kind of ecstasy. The build-up was longer and the release was so much more intense. I let out a huge cry as blood rushed through my skin and I felt the waves of excitement settle in my nipples and my entire body. I wanted nothing more than to let her control me, and my cunt felt as if it were releasing a massive sigh, an exhalation. But it wasn't an exhalation—it was a giant stream of cum-like fluid that shot out of me and onto her face in a glorious moment of sheer abandon.

I had never seen anything like it. I panted and gasped for air. She wiped her face on her sleeve. I apologised. We both laughed. She poured us each a glass of water and I drank mine quickly, as though I had completed a marathon—which, in a way, I had.

"That was incredible. You're incredible." It was difficult to string words together after what had happened.

"What can I say?" she shrugged.

"You're so hot," I said, aware that I had not only lost my cool, but I had lost all composure and intelligence as well.

"You think so? You're not so bad yourself, helper tart."

"What *was* that?"

"What?"

"What you did to me."

"You did it yourself." She smiled, casually, as though this was the most normal thing in the world for her. I had never experienced anything like it. She had opened up a Pandora's box of sexual mystique and all she could offer was this? She was undeniably one of the most frustratingly stoical people I'd ever had the pleasure of meeting.

She sipped at her water, managing, yet again, to appear unfazed by what had transpired between us.

"Well, where did you learn all that?" I knew the question was dumb and I didn't care.

"Learn what?"

"Come on, Sam. That was the best fuck I've ever had."

"Really?" She raised her eyebrows sarcastically.

I nodded, patting down my tousled hair and trying to collect the pieces of my regular self. She tried not to look flattered, but I could tell that she was.

I went over to where she was standing and tried to get her to hold me. Instead, she tied my apron behind my back. I was confused. I brushed up against her, trying to feel for her nipples underneath her shirt. I felt clumsy and awkward—I didn't know what to do to repay her for the best sex I'd ever had. She looked unmoved by my advances. I tried to think rationally, but I was flustered and felt like crawling into bed. I wanted to feel her body against mine. I wanted to rest against her, but I also wanted more of her.

"Take me to your room," I insisted.

"What for?"

"More."

"Can't. Breakfast."

"Oh, fuck it, I'll take some coffee up to the boys myself and tell them that, if they want anything else, they can drag their lazy asses down here and get it themselves."

"But..."

"But what? I've had enough of this. I'm meeting you in your room in five minutes, and you better be there. Do you understand?"

"I thought you were the tart," she said.

"Think again, sir."

Chapter Ten

I whisked upstairs in a fury, carrying a tray with a coffee carafe, two mugs, cream and sugar. My wetness ran down my leg. In any other circumstances, this might have been embarrassing but I was far beyond that now. I didn't care what it took—I was going to feel Sam's skin against mine.

Hal and Timothy were still sleeping when I knocked on Timothy's door. I put the tray down and hurried down to Sam's room. It was much tinier than mine and Hal's, but it looked like home. It felt like her place once she shut the door.

"Where were we?" I started. "Oh, yes. That's right. I was going to take your shirt off and then your pants and then I was going to explore you with my mouth."

She sat on her bed, looking hesitant.

I sat beside her, tossed the ridiculous apron onto her floor and grabbed at her thigh with my hand. This time, I pushed her back. She landed on her mattress and I quickly straddled her. I wasn't expecting this to feel the way it did.

When I'd thought about touching Kelly, I wouldn't have done it like this. Sam brought something out in me. I wanted to be with her as though she were a man—to sit on her and ride her—but it was different than that, too.

Sam, I trusted, would guide me to what she wanted and, more than ever, I was determined to give her everything she wanted and more. I was eager to please her in a way that I had never been eager to please anyone. She took my nipples alternately into her mouth again, and I felt the longing inside me take over. It was as though the whole encounter was dictated by my immense desire to feel that same sense of release, but I also wanted to provide it. She had confessed that she had been watching me and I felt that what she meant was that she wanted me. A solitary life was one thing. Bodies breathing and sweating in close proximity was quite another.

I undid her chef's shirt buttons, which was quite a complex task in the heat of that moment. She watched me the whole time and her stare was intimidating. She wore a white undershirt, which she wanted to keep on. Whatever she wanted, was my only thought. I moved off her for a moment so that I could unzip her jeans. She moaned at this and helped me to pull them off. She pulled off the boxer shorts she wore and I marvelled at how intensely sexual she was, despite all her efforts to eschew my earlier advances. There is something hot about a woman wearing men's underwear. It's that simple. I was completely smitten with the sight.

I wanted to give her what she had given me, so I knelt next to her and mimicked her moves. I placed my finger by her opening but she stopped me, shaking her head.

"Not like that," she said.

"Then how?"

She grabbed my hair again and pulled my very willing lips to her pussy. She was even wetter than me, and, as soon as I felt the softness of her skin on my mouth combined with her firm grip on my hair, I became hyper-aroused, incapable of even stopping myself. Her clitoris hardened and she moaned and gasped. I wanted to stay there forever. I wanted to feel her orgasm against my lips. But it wasn't about what I wanted.

She pulled me away and reached into her drawer. She pulled out a purple dildo shaped like a cock. She also had a harness, which she put on. Then she strapped the cock onto herself. I was floored at the sight. Then she turned me onto my knees. I pulled at her pillows and placed them underneath me. Then I grabbed on to the edge of her mattress, anxious to feel her enter me.

Gripping my hips firmly, as she had when we were in the kitchen, she carefully nudged her cock inside me. I was thrilled at the foreignness and familiarity as her massive presence made me moan again. She grabbed both of my shoulders and I arched my back, securing myself literally as her pedestal, balancing both our foundations. She thrust deeper and deeper into me and became more and more tense. I loved hearing her shortness of breath and feeling her stern hold on my hips and ass. I was still so sensitive from our previous encounter and her thrusting sent me over the top once more. I'm not convinced that I would have come if it hadn't been for how extraordinarily aroused I became at the idea of her orgasm. Building closer and closer to it, she held me tighter and tighter and finally let out a roar of a moan, which my body had no choice but to follow. My sensitive clit gave way to yet another exaggerated explosion of an orgasm as we both moaned and cried and screamed in harmony for what felt like an eternity.

She crashed on top of me, her still-hard rubber cock sliding gently out of my more than satisfied cunt. She eased herself beside me and lay next to me, stroking my skin peacefully. I had not expected to see this side of her, but I was pleasantly surprised by her gentleness.

Her face was flushed and sweat still poured from her brow as she smiled at me. "Thanks," she said. "I needed that."

I didn't say, "You're welcome" — that would have been too strange. Instead, I stroked her cheek a little as we both drifted off into a light catnap. I was satisfied with myself for having won her over, but somehow it was mildly disappointing, in the sense that I had learned how much I wanted to explore her but, inevitably, we would have no future together. We were to dock in less than twenty-four hours and she'd go back to her solitary existence, and I'd go on to my life of indiscreet discretion.

We woke up several hours later, both feeling guilty, and jumped out of bed, got dressed and bolted to the kitchen. Hal had beaten us there, and was happily stirring a steaming pot of lobster bisque.

"I'm sorry, Mr Broughton," Sam pleaded. I'd never heard her address Hal as anything other than Hal.

"Please. Please, Sam. Hal." He stirred thoughtfully. "Jeez, you can fuck a man's wife but you can't call him by his first name?" he said, shocking us. His blushing revealed that we were not alone in our astonishment.

Sam obviously didn't know what to say, so I said, "Pleasing a wife is hard to do, and this was one quality fuck, Hal. This woman deserves a promotion."

Then I walked up to him and hugged him from behind, my messy hair still flying in all directions. I took the wooden spoon from him and stirred. He smiled at me and shook his head.

"I'll see you outside on the deck, Hal." I kissed his cheek in a proper, wife-like fashion.

He nodded and marched up to the deck.

"I think you're right," Sam said.

"About what?"

"You *will* be the last woman Hal ever brings on board the yacht. Nicely handled."

I nodded. Then winked.

* * * *

Sam was much friendlier for the rest of that day. I didn't know if it was because I had managed to thrill her, or because this was our last day on board her home. It didn't much matter. I enjoyed every minute of it. That night, I slept in her room with her, lying pressed up against her with her arm around me. It was the perfect end to our perfect trip.

The next morning, when we were just hours from the marina, Timothy broke down. His wife had factored in my mind primarily as a source of leverage when he teased me. She had not been, in my consciousness, a whole, complicated person with a history of her own. I hardly even had a mental image of her.

Timothy smoked on the deck, looking out at the horizon, and I couldn't help but feel a sombre desperation emanating from him that wasn't usually there. He wasn't crying in the usual sense, with tears. It was more like his whole body—his spirit—was crying and it was a difficult thing for me to see, after the way I had come to know him during the past week.

I stood beside him, not looking at him, because I felt as if he were ashamed of being so obvious about his feelings. I put my hand on his forearm.

"I married her to do the right thing." He turned to me.

I hadn't heard him speak of children, so I wondered what he meant.

"Right thing?" I repeated.

"Years ago," he started. "She was pregnant. Her parents didn't want me to marry her but they were even less fond of the idea of a bastard in the family."

"I didn't think you had kids."

"She miscarried after the wedding."

"I'm sorry."

"I'm not. She would have been a terrible mother, and look at me. I'm not exactly model father material."

"A kid could do worse, Timothy."

"Anyway, her parents have always resented me for it, like I had planned it, you know? Like I had gotten her pregnant on purpose and then gotten her *un*pregnant on purpose."

"And her?"

"Oh, she resents me every day of her life. I'm not the kind of man she was supposed to be with, if you know what I mean. She was supposed to wind up with a fellow like Hal, you know—someone of good breeding."

"You're pretty refined," I offered, knowing that he'd feed me the same lie if need be.

"Oh, it's not about that. Look at you. You've got the look, the manners. They'll sniff it out on you, though. Aristocrats have noses for us intruders."

"Like you, I guess," I said. "How could you tell? About me, I mean?"

"You do belong, Julie. That's the thing. The only obstacle is making them believe that you do."

"How do you do that?"

"Lie. I mean, do what you did with Hal."

I looked out at the ocean. The truth is that the only obstacle to feeling worthy is mindset. I was worlds away from where I had been born and where I'd grown up, and I could have spent my time trying to create a similar life to my parents', but I had already decided that I wasn't going to.

I thought about what they might think if they had been there with me at that moment. My mom wouldn't have known how to behave. She'd never had anything come to her easily. Her whole life had been about settling for very little. In a way, I reasoned, it was her own fault for never having believed she was capable of more. My dad might have made something better for himself by now, but I had no intention of finding out. What would he have said to me now? Most fathers wouldn't be proud of daughters like me, but I think my dad would have said I came upon my fortune honestly. He'd sold the best things he had— his labour, his management skills and his apples. He'd done okay. The bankruptcy hadn't been his fault—the industry had been in steady decline and, in spite of having too many bills and not enough resources, he'd managed to leave a decent insurance policy. He'd been a decent provider for us. Idaho is a different world. People just don't aim big the way they do elsewhere. It's different. And people don't grow up with a lot of property and generations of money, like Hal and his friends in Virginia.

My sister, on the other hand — I didn't even dare to think what had become of her. Had she cashed the insurance cheque and left? Or had she and Tommy taken the plunge and salvaged the life my parents had wanted for her? Every time I thought to contact her, I remembered how utterly judgemental she was and thought of how intolerable she would find my life, and it made me too angry to consider finding her, though I couldn't help but wonder what had become of her plan to marry Tommy.

I wondered what kind of family Timothy came from. I sort of figured they must have been something like my own clan, but as we stood on the deck, leaning out towards the vast ocean, it seemed like the wrong kind of question to ask. Besides, it didn't much matter where he'd come from. It mattered more where he was going and how we were all going to deal with his wife.

"What's her name?" I finally asked.

"Francine. Francine Jean."

"Wow. It even rhymes."

"Yeah. Everything in her life fits so perfectly together."

"Except you, you big stud. I take it she doesn't know about your philandering."

"She knows about a couple of women. She has no idea about the men."

"There were more?"

"Than Hal? Sure. Lots." He smiled. "I was always careful. But, come on, why do you think I became a travelling businessman?"

"Good point. You know, I don't even know what you do, Timothy."

"Neither does my wife. It's best that way, wouldn't you agree?"

"Whatever you say. How do you think it'll be to be around your wife and me and Hal? You think Hal will feel weird?"

"First off, if she thinks anything's going on that shouldn't be, she'll assume it's between you and me. I'm not worried about Hal because, once we're on land, I think he'll be dying to pretend like this never happened—until some cute gardener shows up on your veranda one morning while you're out. You know what I mean."

"And you? How will it be for you?"

"I don't even think about that anymore. I've just got used to it. Her ways. Hal's one lucky, lucky fellow. It takes quite a woman to be with a guy like Hal."

"I don't think you're giving him enough credit. I really do love Hal, you know. And I'm proud of him for coming to terms with who he is. It might sound somewhat pretentious, given that I've known him for all of a month now, but I think it's a beautiful thing that's going on here."

"Oh, to be so young and so wise." He grinned.

"What do you mean?"

"You know what freedom is. My wife has no idea. And look at me. It's too late for me."

"It's not, Timothy."

"Okay, Pollyanna."

"Well..."

"Well, what? You don't get it. It's been two decades. I've already put in my time with her parents, waiting for their inheritance, her telling me what to do all those years. She calls the shots, you know. The one with the money always does."

"Not Hal." I smiled.

"Don't get cocky. It's the worst mistake you can make. You think someone loves you for you. Hal needs you right now. If he doesn't in the future, well, all I'm saying is, don't get cocky."

He pulled out a cigarette. "She even pays for these. Probably hopes I'm going to get cancer and die."

"So why doesn't she just divorce you, if you're so worthless?"

"Because that's not the way the world works. Think about it. Why would she? She can do everything she wants already. She likes to think she controls my life and the worst part is that she actually does. She loves it. Why would she change that? God, making me miserable brings her such joy." He chuckled. "Crazy."

Then he really laughed. It was the kind of desperate laughter that suggests all last resorts have already been taken. I was no longer doubtful that they had. Timothy had probably exhausted all options. For all I knew, he'd toyed with the idea of killing her for his inheritance. She'd probably had some kind of clause built into her will to protect herself from just such a misfortune. Yes, the man who stood in front of me was like a dog on a very familiar leash who knew exactly what he could and could not get away with. He wasn't the big man I'd thought he was. He was a shell of what he could have been. I wouldn't be like that, I told myself. I would never let Hal do that to me. It wouldn't happen, anyway. It was the unfair disparity between being a pretty young woman and a middle-aged man. We were measured differently.

It was good for us to talk about these things. But talking is double-edged. Too much talking leads to friendship. Timothy was about to go back to his prison. All I could do was to give him a decent farewell.

"Forget about her. She's still hours away. Don't let her ruin your afternoon." I grabbed his cock through his pants.

He jumped. I hadn't ever been quite so forward, and it had started to seem inappropriate, the way our conversation was going.

"Oh, come on, Timothy. We'll always be confidants, but who knows when we'll get to be lovers again?"

"You're incorrigible, Julie," he said, shaking his head. Then he leaned in and kissed my neck. I loved that feeling.

He sat me up on the ledge of the deck. I opened my legs to make room for him in between them. It was perfect. The sun was beating down on us. The wind was in my hair. It was a little bit chilly—not chilly enough to be a deterrent, but chilly enough to make touching each other extra exciting and inviting. He unzipped my summer jacket. The breeze made my nipples immediately hard and he stared at them. Poor thing. This would be the last time he'd see them for a while, and I could feel him taking in the sight of them, the touch and feel of them. He was committing me to memory, like a soldier going off to war. For me, it was great. I love that kind of attention. If I hadn't been so caught up in the moment, I could have taken on his nostalgia as well.

I used my legs to pull him in tight and felt his bulge against my crotch. I had savoured this before, but I felt like time was running out on us and I was eager to take my share of him. Also, Hal was still downstairs, as were Sam and the captain and first mate, and I wanted this to be between me and Timothy.

He squeezed on my nipples between the cloth of my shirt and my bra and still I jumped the way he had when the sensation shot through me, straight to my clit. I felt as if it was game over at that point—I just wanted him to take me right there on the deck, free in the afternoon sun.

I unzipped his pants and stroked his cock out of the opening. I was, thankfully, wearing a skirt. I jumped to my feet, took my coat off, whipped my panties off in a frenzy and sat back up on the ledge. He lifted my shirt up and I lifted my arms to encourage him to take it off completely. He did, and placed it on top of my jacket. I unclasped my bra, then tossed it on top of the tiny pile of clothes, grabbed him by the neck and guided his lips to my nipple. His tongue circled my areola and I gulped, wanting so badly for him to be inside me. He wasn't in as much of a hurry as me. I thought he was taking his time so that he could really do it justice, but I was so wet and so willing that I ran out of patience. I stroked his cock with my right hand as I held onto him with my left. He pulled a condom from his back pocket. I fumbled with the wrapper, cursing it in my frustration. They can send a man to the moon, they can clone sheep, and still condoms are such a pain to open. But my will empowered me. I put it on him quickly and just as fast, I guided him, practically pulled him, to my awaiting cunt.

Just the feel of his cock at the entrance was enough to make me hold my breath in utter anticipation of the pleasure to come. Timothy was one heck of a well-built man. His cock was beautifully balanced. Its girth to length ratio was something of a golden mean. He had the perfect penis. The head created just enough sensation as he travelled deeper into me. I wrapped my legs around him and squeezed them together, pulling us closer to each other. He wrapped his big hands around my ass and held my hips in place as he began to thrust in and out of me.

I was in awe. We hadn't had a private moment thus far, and I was surprised at how manly he was. It seemed like a bad kind of judgement on my part. It wasn't. He was equally as hot when he was kissing Hal, but being with me alone brought something else out in him. He seemed somehow more brutal, more in control, and I liked that. I loved the roughness with which he pushed himself into me. I was stuck between the ledge and his body, his cock deep inside me, his hands holding me still. It was as if I was his receptacle and I loved the thought of it. I wanted so badly to feel him come inside me.

He was so burly — the observation just came to me. I grabbed his neck and pulled myself up on him. strong hands. He cupped my ass cheeks with his hands and I followed his lead perfectly. He lifted me up, and my skirt crinkled up in between us as he pulled me away from the ledge. Cradled in his embrace, I found myself in the middle of the deck. Timothy was holding me, his cock pumping in and out of me. The feeling of his arms tensing, his muscles contracting as he pulled up and down as if he were bench pressing me was enough to send me to the edge. Both of us.

I leant back as he kept thrusting, and he took my left nipple in his mouth, keeping the rhythm. I could no longer hold myself back. The contractions of my orgasm were so intense and he moaned in pleasure at my tightness. I thought that he, too, was going to come, but he didn't. In fact, his face showed a different kind of determination. I was almost a little scared. I became so sensitive just after I came, and he was still holding me like that, like his receptacle and, even though I pushed his mouth away from my left nipple, he greedily sucked on my right one instead.

My poor cunt was so sensitive, and I got goose bumps because he wouldn't stop. I didn't care, though. I didn't want him to stop. I loved the breeze on my almost-naked body. I loved the smell we made together. The fragrance of my orgasm and the look on his face were so intense.

We paused to change positions. I grabbed him by the waist when he looked as if he was about to lose control. If this was going to be our last time together, I wanted a little more of him. He panted and sweated profusely. It really was quite the workout for him, and I was thrilled to be his equipment. He put me back down on the ledge in a sitting position and withdrew his cock from me. He was rock solid, a glorious sight. I only wished that I was capable of fucking for hours. I didn't want this to stop. I felt insatiable.

I turned over so I was on my hands and knees on top of the bench cabinet that housed safety equipment. He moaned in gratitude at the ingenuity of the position. Obviously, it was exactly what he wanted. He grabbed my hips and thrust himself into me again. The angle was different and he felt even larger. He really was massive inside me. I had felt it before but somehow, like this, it was as though he could just plough farther and farther into me. I loved the feeling that it was him doing this to me, that I was his plaything. He needed that, but I needed it more.

In that moment, with his hands around my hips and his cock deep inside me, I realised that I had agreed to take such an active role with Hal. I was the choreographer, the operator. I liked that. I loved Hal. But I also loved being passive. The way I was with Sam, but different. I loved this feeling. There was something about it that was so familiar, it felt as though it was inscribed upon my psyche. It was a way that men and women seemed to have related to each other for millennia. Not sensual, not loving, but animalistic. It was perfect.

Timothy eased his hands onto my shoulders and pulled me backwards, farther onto him. I arched my back upwards and he rounded the bend of my chest with his left hand as his right hand came around and stroked my breasts in the warm afternoon air. I felt the breeze against my nipples.

He hardened even more, although I hadn't thought it was possible. He pulled me back and forth so hard now, and started to moan loudly. The primal cries behind me and the feeling that I could do nothing to stop him from coming inside me were too much for me to take, and I felt another orgasm grow deep in my belly. As he thrust back and forth, I bucked myself back onto him with all of my strength. If I hadn't already come before, it would have been too much for me to handle but, as it was, I felt the energy build and build. Just as he released, I started to contract around his cock, which sent him into further utopia. He was so loud—I had never heard him and Hal be that loud—and I threw my own cries into the mix and came violently with him. We were in perfect sync, him giving me the last few thrusts as my cunt released its tension.

Timothy let my body go and I sat on the ledge, limp from exhaustion. I leaned my cheek against his chest and listened to his still-racing heartbeat. I would have stayed like that for as long as I could, but time was limited and we both knew it.

"I'll miss you, Julie. I'll miss you a lot," Timothy said.

"I'm not going anywhere."

I knew that wasn't the point. I knew it was more about him leaving, his wife coming, the whole new situation that we all had on our hands now.

* * * *

We approached the marina mid afternoon. Francine Jean had driven for hours to meet her husband, undoubtedly hoping to catch him disembarking a vessel stocked with girls. She seemed somewhat relieved as she stood in her crisp white dress with her giant white sun hat and her dark glasses, waving to us from the shore. She was beautiful and stylish and I felt ignorant for having taken Timothy's story of her as fact. She was delicate of frame and graceful and deserving of a husband who adored her. At least, that was what I believed when I saw her at a distance.

Up close, she exuded the kind of high-maintenance air that I could only hope to portray. She kissed everyone on the cheek, calling each of us 'sugar'. I didn't know what to do so I obliged, mimicking her behaviour.

"Why, Hal, wherever did you find this precious lady?" she cooed at him.

"I'd say it was a fortunate chance encounter in San Francisco," Hal started, "but I actually believe it was fate."

"Oh, how sweet." She turned her sights on me.

Timothy packed his suitcase into the back of his wife's expensive convertible. He approached us and put his arm around Francine Jean in an effort to appear affectionate. Instead, it appeared forced and uncomfortable, as though she was made of porcelain and not meant for touching.

"Well, I guess this is it, then," he said. "You two lovebirds had best be off. We wouldn't want to get in the way of Julie falling in love with Florida. Anyway, it's a bit of a drive from here, isn't that right, Francine Jean?"

"I'll say," she uttered, as though she had been terribly inconvenienced by coming to get him. No one mentioned that it was at her own insistence.

Timothy and I kissed cheek to cheek in front of Francine Jean and Hal. Hal and Timothy shook hands. Francine Jean and I shook hands.

"Pleasure to meet you," I said to her. "I do hope we see you at the wedding."

"The pleasure's all mine, dear, and I wouldn't miss it."

It was fake, phony and full of lies. But this was my new life and I wasn't about to feel dismayed about it.

"I forgot something on board," I told the group as they slowly meandered towards Francine Jean's perfect little car. I ran back out on the dock and called Sam. She poked her head up, then climbed onto the deck.

"Bye, Sam," I whispered.

"Bye, yourself," she said. "And good luck with everything."

"You too."

Chapter Eleven

Strawberry Hill

Hal's chauffeur, Stanley, picked us up at the harbour. We spent the better part of the afternoon and evening driving towards a bed and breakfast resort that Hal frequented when he made this familiar trek. The next morning, we drove to Halifax County, which, Hal said, he hoped I liked as it was the gateway to my new home. Even in the car, our dynamic was different. We were silent for the most part. I stared out of the window at the landscape, which was far more lush than I had imagined. I think Hal missed Timothy already, or else he missed the freedom that the last week had given him. I reminisced about the best sexual encounters I'd ever had.

The air was warm and lush and the nature quite different from any I had seen so far. My home town had been rich with trees as well, but with the kind of overgrowth of the unattended. When we crossed the state line, I noticed that everything in Virginia seemed pruned and intentional. Leafy vines covered massive trees. We passed rolling hills and the sun beamed down on the grassy meadows. It was like being in a fairytale.

On the evening of our second driving day, we approached the driveway of Strawberry Hill, Hal's mansion. The scene was extraordinary. In fact, with its Greek pillars, even the servant's quarters were impressive. This place was a relic from a bygone era, something I'd never imagined I would see with my own eyes. As we drove past the first set of buildings, I understood that I had been looking to the side when I should have been looking straight ahead. In front of us was the largest mansion I had ever seen. Brooding like a Greek hero, the mansion intimidated even me, who had been so intent on being nonchalant.

I realised that Hal's uniqueness was an opportunity for me to receive the kind of pleasure most men were not capable of giving me. Most men, I figured, would never be able to provide a woman with this kind of luxury. If they were, there would undoubtedly be a hefty price tag attached in some form or another. With Hal, although we each had ends of a bargain to uphold, I felt as though this lifestyle was much more than adequate compensation for my loyalty. Hal needed a beautiful woman on his arm and I was determined to give him everything his heart desired, and more. I was more than the perfect job applicant — I was making a career of being his partner.

Upon our arrival at his mansion in Virginia, he showed me to my room, a flawlessly decorated, massive bedroom done up in ornate style. Everywhere my eyes focused, there were priceless antiques, baroque fixtures and marble flooring. This was not just any old heritage plantation. This was opulence that I had not known existed. Growing up in Idaho, I had set my sights on what I'd seen in the stories – the rich Texan mansions, the Californian millionaires. Virginia's estates resonated with old money. The original, cold-hearted entrepreneurs had started here. This place had been built long before plebes had worked the land in my northern neck of the woods.

What would these people think if they knew the truth about me? I could understand everything Timothy had said now. And I knew that, no matter what Hal might reassuringly tell me, if I was going to survive and thrive in this environment, I'd have to lie. I'd have to pretend. I'd have to become Francine Jean's younger, prettier doppelgänger.

A couple of days of glorious rest later, Hal approached me during my morning tea. I was to adorn myself with yet another new wardrobe befitting my stature as the lady of the house. To this, I agreed with my usual attempt at aloofness. It was, after all, a matter of course that he would do anything to please me. It was a matter of course that I'd have everything my heart desired. It was in the terms of the contract.

I was slowly settling into the realisation that this was my reality. After the wild times at sea, a couple of weeks of rest suited me perfectly. I delighted in exploring the county and Stanley was an excellent guide. The only trouble was that on most days I was alone. I'd always thought that I wanted money above all things. I'd believed that a life of luxury equalled happiness but I soon discovered that, more than wealth, I valued companionship. And with Hal preoccupied with business, and Stanley an exceptionally boring man, I began to wonder where I might meet the other hypothetical lovers that Hal and

I had agreed to enjoy. Certainly, there would not be a lot of excitement around Strawberry Hill.

Just when I was beginning to wonder whether I could really be happy with this arrangement, Simon entered my life. One day, at tea, Hal told me about him.

"Julie, I really must insist that you take advantage of my tailor. He's fresh out of fashion school and ambitious. Find some new projects to occupy his time. Surely it will be more interesting for him than making suits for an old man."

"Hal, you're not old." I sipped my Earl Grey. "Where do I find him?"

"He'll come around at two. I'm sure you need some new clothes."

"Fabulous."

"Then it's settled. He'll meet you in the boudoir. I should warn you — he's handsome." He smiled. "Well, I'm off."

That was how things went at Strawberry Hill. Hal had his business to attend to, which, from what I could gather, consisted of making appearances. I would eventually be expected to attend social functions on his arm, but it was too much to ask of a belle to do so on her first week. Organising smooth inheritance probably also required a great deal of charisma, and Hal was very distracted during those first weeks back home. I could sympathise. Coming into the estate as an outsider presented me with a certain disbelief. The threat of the government confiscating it from him must have been a nightmare. Once accustomed to this kind of living, as Hal had been his whole life, since he spent all of his summers here, nothing else would be impressive. Not the fancy hotel suites, not the most extravagant homes on the west coast. Nothing.

At two o'clock, I met Simon the tailor in my dressing lounge. Hal's warning had been accurate. He was a strapping young man — a design student, apparently — who made his living sewing for Virginia's best dressed. Hal adored him. I immediately understood why.

When he entered the room, he fumbled and accidentally dropped his sketchbook. Instead of simply picking up the fallen drawings, he apologised profusely and started a hilarious chain reaction that culminated in his bumping his head on the coffee table. Why is it that nervousness piques my interest?

"You have to forgive me, ma'am, for my clumsiness. I have only worked for men before," he said, as he held the measuring tape around my waist, taking preliminary peeks at what was to become his new oeuvre.

"Hmm, I suppose this must be awkward for you, then." I took the measuring tape from him and lowered it around my hips.

His cough expressed his stress as he recorded my measurements in his notebook. He struck me as inexperienced and sweet. He was just the kind of well-behaved young man that a woman could really enjoy. He seemed determined to say and do the right thing all the time.

"This must be intolerable." I placed the tape around my bust and motioned for him to take it from me. He clasped the tape and came close to see the number. "You poor thing," I said. Then I laughed.

He feigned amusement.

There is something so titillating about inexperienced men. Simon was the perfect specimen. His bookish fumbling and lack of social grace told me that, if he had been with a woman before, it had not been an affirming experience. His gentle hands almost shook as he wrote. I could not help but play with him. What could be the harm in a little innocent flirtation?

"Simon?"

"Yes?"

"Do you think I'm pretty?"

"Yes, ma'am. Absolutely."

"I don't believe you."

"Pardon?"

"I don't believe you. Prove it."

"Um... I'm not sure what you mean."

"Well, you said you think I'm pretty. I want you to prove it," I said, squinting ever so slightly. I just wanted to hint at something dirty, not actually come on to him. In his volatile state, an actual advance would have been devastating.

He cleared his throat. "I'm not sure Mr Broughton would approve."

"Oh? And why not? How were you going to prove my prettiness to me?" I pouted.

"Um..." He had no idea what to do, and I enjoyed watching him squirm. I was just having fun but his expression suggested this was torture for him.

"I think we should leave Hal out of this, don't you?" I took the notebook he was clinging to so naïvely and tossed it onto the floor. He stared at me as if I were the most wicked and crazy woman he had ever met, and I loved it. He was so deathly afraid of upsetting Hal — and even more afraid of abandoning his etiquette — that his face became pale, like a Victorian lady's.

I pushed him slightly, and he fell backwards onto my boudoir's velvet ottoman.

"I'm not sure..."

"What, Simon? You're not sure this is appropriate? You're not sure if you'll lose your contract with Hal?" I paused. "Or is it that you're not sure I'm pretty?"

"Oh, you're very pretty. I'm definitely sure of that."

"Then why don't you want to prove it to me?" I pouted. It had been a couple of weeks without any sexual attention and I was hungry for something tasty.

I climbed on top of him where he was seated. I straddled his lap and felt his throbbing presence between my legs. "Oh, I see… You do want to prove it to me. You're just afraid to say it. Is that true, Simon?"

"Yes, ma'am."

I jumped from his lap and gained my composure. Standing in front of him, I towered over him. Then I slapped him. Hard. Across the face with my open hand. "I cannot tolerate fearful men in my home."

"Ma'am?"

"You heard me. If you are too afraid of Hal or me to tell me how you really feel, then you might as well leave now, or I will personally see to it that your position here is terminated."

"I'm not afraid." His voice suggested otherwise, but the young man was coming to his senses, aware that I wanted to play a game with him. That was all this was—just a game of cat and mouse—though, like a good predator, I pounced when he least expected it.

"I don't believe you," I insisted.

He stood up. He was taller than me, and slim. Despite his scholarly physique, he was handsome and exuded an artistic flair. He was unlike any of the men I'd met on the road or at Carla's, and he was nothing at all like the guys in Idaho. I could tell just from his choice to wear corduroy slacks and a loose-fitting, white linen shirt. He stared into my eyes, then grasped both of my arms with his strong hands.

I was momentarily stunned as our dynamic shifted. It had been a while since a man had handled me this way, and I savoured the familiarity of feeling small in someone's arms. He pulled me close. Our faces almost touching, he whispered, "Julie, you are a beautiful woman. I can hardly control myself in your presence, if I must be honest."

"You shouldn't have to," I said, and closed my eyes. His lips met mine and our kiss resonated deep inside me. I could feel his hardness as he pulled my body flush with his own. I broke away from Simon, walked calmly to the door, turned the key, then turned on my heels. I could feel myself moisten with each step I took towards him.

Even the most cultivated creative type has an animalistic side. I was about to encounter Simon, unbridled. It had been too long that I had waited. The adventures with Sam and Timothy and Hal had been fascinating, but I was in dire need of a ravishing union.

I tore at Simon's buttoned shirt. He immediately shed his pants, his undergarments, everything. As he stood there, exposed, I felt the desire to intimidate the poor young man a little more.

"What makes you think you can have me?" I asked. He looked confused. "Hmm? Mr Tailor? What makes you think you're good enough to fuck the lady of the house?"

I even surprised myself with my tone. But Simon played along, perfect prey that he was.

"I don't think I'm good enough." His tone was meek.

"You don't *think* you are?"

"I know I'm not, ma'am. I'm not good enough for you."

"That's right, Tailor Boy. Now get down on your knees."

He knelt down. Crouched on my floor, he kissed my feet. He caressed my ankles with his soft hands and I sat down on my ottoman, fully clothed in front of my naked admirer. His dedication emanated from every part of his body. I could not help but feel adored. Something told me I could get used to having Simon around.

He stroked and caressed my left foot as I brought my toe to his mouth. He engulfed it with his soft, warm tongue, which was exactly the fellatio I craved. His suction became more and more prominent as I pushed and pulled my toe in and out of his mouth. With my right foot, I stroked the ever-growing bulge between his legs, which made him moan in delight. He slid his tongue between my toes and I cradled his now throbbing hardness with my other foot until we were both in dire need of relief. I recalled the image I had of Kelly — Mistress Veronica — and let myself feel the longing I still had for her.

* * * *

Simon and I had an excellent understanding. He was happy to design and sew and cater to my needs. In return, I toyed with him every time I felt like it. It was the perfect flattering union. I couldn't have planned it better. Simon worked busily, compiling a late summer wardrobe of light dresses and pretty blouses for me. I perused fashion magazines and picked out fabrics and shoes and accessories. His job was to say 'yes' to me. It wasn't an exaggeration to say that Simon became the hobby that occupied my time in those first couple of months at Strawberry Hill.

Hal could tell how much I was enjoying the arrangement.

"That Simon, he's quite the terrific tailor, wouldn't you say, darling?" he asked me one night, in his study.

I loved Hal. We were so easy around each other. It was easy to love him and easy to get along with him. We liked the same lifestyle and he never saw himself as my keeper, even though he was.

"Simon is excellent," I confirmed, lying on his beautiful cherry-wood-trimmed sofa, reading my magazines while he sat at his desk with his cup of tea and paperwork. Many evenings were spent like this. It was hard not to love his study. It was better than an office, with its brick fireplace and bear rug, its antique furniture and old style lighting.

"Simon and I are preparing a surprise for you, dear."

"For me? Does it involve nudity and a bottle of oil?"

He chuckled quietly. Whenever we were alone together, Hal felt comfortable to voice things he would never say in public.

"No, darling, nothing so dashing. I think you'll like it, though."

He was so dapper, Hal. I loved to do nice things for him. This surprise—the jade dildo and my perfectly fitted harness—was my latest obsession. It might not be the kind of surprise Hal was up for, but it was the kind of thing I felt was my duty. I just couldn't resist.

He smiled at my coyness and we went back to our silent, solitary activities. I really loved him even though we hadn't consummated in that way...yet. I often thought about it. I wondered if he did, too. We had sort of fallen into a pattern of not fucking because that was what seemed most natural. It seemed as if we shouldn't because his preferences lay elsewhere. But I became intent on the idea. After all, we cared about each other. It was dangerous for me to start thinking of him in that way and I knew it. Our relationship had already reached the pinnacle of intimacy because we had been sleeping in the same bed, regularly, for months.

There is something about waking up in bed together that is inherently more private than sharing bodily fluids. I let Hal see me in what I think of as the most compromising position—sleep followed by bed hair. It was one thing to show off my body and my flexibility, to leave lovers wanting more or, even in the case of Sam, to leave them confused or at least with a mental image of my physical nudity. But Hal knew what I looked like naked in the real sense of it—devoid of all airs. He knew what it felt like to hold me, to feel my arms wrapped around him at night. He knew what I sounded like when I slept, whether I snored or not. He was always such a gentleman, so I never believed him when he told me I didn't snore, but how would I know? The only other person I could ask was Kelly and those days had been different. Hal and I, though, we had something. It was a kind of closeness, more than a platonic relationship, more than a brother-sister style relationship. We weren't asexual. In fact, we loved telling each other about our escapades and we had been involved with the same lover, so we couldn't have pretended not to notice each other in that way. I didn't want to put our closeness at risk with my harness plan. I couldn't bear the thought of Hal's rejection. I feared it terribly, which was why it had taken me so long to get Simon to make the harness. But as our wedding night approached, I felt that there would be something satisfying about Hal and I being able to express ourselves together.

One morning, as the sun shone through the white curtains, I felt his morning erection against me. I didn't do anything about it, though part of me wanted so badly to slip underneath the covers and to take him in my mouth. I couldn't do that kind of thing with him. He wouldn't like it. In fact, I was quite sure he would have to be extremely turned on if he was ever going to let me use the jade dildo on him. I might even have to plan it in conjunction with a visit from Timothy or one of the new boys of which Hal was so fond. But that idea saddened me. I wanted it to be between the two of us. I wanted to be able to seduce him myself. It was the ultimate challenge.

Maybe what he needed, or what *I* needed, was more masculine signifiers, I thought as he put his still sleeping head on my chest. I lay there propped up on his pillows with my arms folded behind my back, and he nuzzled into me. Conventionally, our postures were the reversal of what our genders dictated, which only led me to further think about the possibility. Maybe I should take Simon shopping. Maybe I needed cologne. Maybe I would look great in tweed pants and a white collared shirt and a tie. Maybe I should learn to smoke a pipe. I smiled at the idea. It was no longer about Hal. I should feel as comfortable to do that as anything. Why not?

I'd been laying there in my private thoughts, looking out of the window, when Hal woke up. He looked at me.

"I can't wait to be your wife," I said. "Let's do it soon."

"If it were up to me, I'd bring the minister out today. We could do it right here, right now."

"Minister? Like from a church?"

"Is there any other kind?"

"I hope so. Hal, I'm hardly a believer."

"Oh," he said. "Well, what would you like?"

"How about a pagan ritual?"

"Your absolute disregard for tradition is very charming."

"What's not traditional about paganism?" I asked sarcastically. "After all, it's been around a lot longer."

"I prefer a minister, dear," Hal said. "For the sake of the guest of honour."

"Who?"

"My benefactor. The reason for the wedding, the owner of Strawberry Hill and all of its surrounding acres."

"Why have you never mentioned this before?"

"In good time, Julie. We're still just getting to know each other."

"Oh."

There was an awkward silence and I realised that Hal was not going to offer any more information on the matter. I asked, "This arrangement isn't just about us, is it?"

"No, it's a little more complicated, I'm afraid. Let's just say you're the missing piece of the puzzle."

"I am?" I was still confused.

"So I insist on a real minister. I hope you can find it in your heart to cooperate with that plan." Hal looked at me over his reading glasses.

I settled into the calm awareness that what we were engaged in was unfathomable by the church. For that reason, there was no need to feel hypocritical. We were free spirits who were marrying for the sake of the state. If Hal felt it best that the church be involved, then who was I to interject? I wasn't here to make a religious statement. I wasn't even here to enter the sanctimonious union of marriage in its ideal form. I was here because I loved Hal, I was ready to commit to him and I didn't need God's approval for that.

"Let's have one of those lovely fall weddings," I urged.

"It might seem too soon, too contrived," Hal argued.

"I thought sooner would be better than later... For you, I mean."

"It is, but I've managed to buy myself some more time. It looks suspicious when a man of my age, and in my situation..."

"Hal, you're second guessing yourself. There's nothing to be secretive about. People fall in love all the time. It's quick. It's passionate. It's perfectly normal," I assured him.

"You don't know my benefactor. Why not let yourself behave like a proper kept woman and let me be in charge, dear?"

I looked at him, baffled. Had I not been behaving like a kept woman? I was unnerved by his secrecy but he was right. It'd be best to let him worry about it.

For good order's sake, we had to make a big event of our big event. We invited all of Hal's associates. We hired photographers and caterers, planners and extra servers. Simon took a week away from Strawberry Hill to personally pick up and escort my wedding dress back home. He had to go all the way to New York City, to one of the world's finest bridal boutiques to pick up my custom gown. Or so he said, but I'd never heard of a successful American company that did not use the postal service or a courier.

I did my part and focused on making Simon very busy. He had to tailor a new tuxedo for Hal, and we both browsed catalogues and magazines for cuff links befitting the situation. No expense was spared.

Chapter Twelve

Throughout the planning, the most important accessory I could think of was my cock. I wanted what Sam had had. But I wanted the best that money could buy. Simon had listened to all my fantasies. The best part about him was that he listened not just as a tailor, but as a lover. I'd started to visit his studio. I called on him to give me one last fitting of the leather harness. It felt so good around my hips. The top of the leather came down in a heart shape in between my ass cheeks, and it stayed snug against my skin even with the beautiful jade cock at the front. He had hand-stitched the piece together. He had ordered the custom cock straight from a jade dealer in Beijing. It really was the finest package money could buy.

"What do you think?" I asked Simon as I emerged, naked, from behind his lacquered room divider. I was naked with my giant erection. His eyes almost came right out of his head.

"You look amazing," he whispered, then gulped. I had managed to make him uncomfortable yet again. Simon was so darling and shy. I almost couldn't help myself but go to extra trouble to make him nervous. I flipped my long hair out over my shoulders and licked my lips. He stood facing me, awkward, not knowing whether to avert his eyes or to ogle me.

"Come here, my boy."

He walked over to me.

"Kneel down, sweetheart." I said. He stood stiff, as though he hadn't heard what I'd said. Then, like clockwork, he fell to his knees.

"I know you want to," I said, combing my fingers through his hair. "You think I can't tell, but I can. It's too obvious. I know you want to suck my cock."

He nodded in silent appreciation of my bountiful endowment. I really did have the most perfect and massive cock I had ever seen. I stood in front of him, stroking myself. It felt so good to move my palm up and down my shaft. I felt large and powerful and so completely free to express myself. Whether consciously or not, I had wanted to feel this way for as long as I could remember. I thought back to the first time I'd taken Tommy's cock in my mouth, back on my parents' farm, in the orchard. I had been so hidden away. Tommy had been so timid. It was as though he'd been ashamed of enjoying his cock.

Not like me. I was proud. I held my head high as I stroked myself and felt myself getting stiffer. It was in my head, I guessed, but my palm really did register a stiffer cock as I touched myself. My clit sprang to attention in a way that had not happened before. The sensation was just different. I wanted to take my time. I wanted my first blow job. I wanted to fill Simon's mouth with my abundance even if it gagged him and I was quite sure, with my deep-rooted need, that I would gag him.

I pulled his mouth to my cock. He kissed the tip of it and opened his lips. Suddenly I felt contained, totally surrounded by the soft flesh of his mouth. I still had his hair between my fingers and stood standing in front of him as he thrust himself onto me. I guided him with my firm grip. He choked.

"I can't... I can't," he muttered through his gurgling noises.

"You will, Simon," I heard myself say. This experience had brought out something new and refined in me. I loved the way I felt. I grabbed his cowering head and shoved it onto my cock, as though Simon was a catalyst for my pleasure and container of what was to come. Tears started to form in his eyes, as if he were drowning in the sensation of being forced to take the entirety of my cock.

"You want this. I can tell. You need my cock," I told him firmly as he sucked and sucked. Even hearing the words come out of my mouth made my clit harder than it had ever felt. I wanted to fuck him. It was a strange feeling, like being removed from myself and being with myself. I thought of how men had looked at me. That feeling they'd seemed to emit, especially when they'd grabbed me and held me tight and thrust my pelvis up and down on top of theirs or when, in the missionary position, they'd penetrated me, then thrust rhythmically in and out. I had that feeling. Like I wanted to prise Simon apart and get inside him and push myself deeper and deeper into him. I was surprised that one little alteration — a harness and a cock — could make me feel this way. The long-dormant feelings were finally able to come out with this chemical reactor, this most perfect prop.

Simon beckoned for more. Kneeling in front of me, he gave me the most intense pleasure by virtue of his position. He was so lovely. His blond hair and sculpted body made him a most perfect candidate for this household. I didn't know if Hal took advantage of his presence as heartily, but I hoped he did. I could only imagine what their union would look like. Probably a lot like my own.

I pushed Simon onto the floor and placed a cushion under his head. I could no longer deal with the anxiety and excitement of what was happening. I crawled on top of him and placed myself carefully, cock in hand, over his mouth. I stroked my cock while his tongue found my pussy. I felt the need to come on him like I'd never experienced the feeling before. In my mind, I could see a whole army of cocks spewing forth their cum, and I was the sergeant major. I was the one with the most bountiful prize.

I made circles on Simon's mouth as he grasped at my hips. I may have come close to suffocating him a bit—at least, his urgent moans suggested that—and I didn't care much. If it was that dire, he'd struggle harder, I reckoned. I didn't have time for distractions. My cock felt so good in my hand. I felt large and stiff and ready to explode on Simon's face and all I could think of was a fabulous stream of my juices running over him. It was splendid, this kind of urgency, this kind of need. It was so different than coming with something inside me. Internal orgasms felt like pulling in. Whenever I came with a cock inside me, I was convinced that my tightening muscles were pulling on my companion's shaft, bringing him deeper. This was an entirely different sensation.

I was rocking back and forth on Simon's mouth, his nose up against my clit, his stifled moans against my pussy, my hands still grabbing at his hair when I felt the building climax of the greatest feeling ever. He stiffened his tongue just slightly and I pushed one final time against him, then let out a massive, satisfying moan. I knew part of it was my imagination, but it was like coming straight through my cock, covering him with my semen. He was drenched. I pulled away feeling as if I were a sexist pig and he was my little tart. I even smiled at the idea.

I'd never wondered what it was like to be a man before. And just because I'd donned a cock didn't mean I was any closer to understanding. But I did think of myself a little differently. Even the way I looked at Simon was different from how I would ordinarily look — I imagined — after an orgasm. And he just seemed stunned. Minutes went by before we exchanged any words at all. I bent down and he held me to his chest. It was oddly comforting to be held after sex — another thing that made me feel different. I felt like I could doze off into the most perfect sleep with him stroking my hair as he was.

"Oh, Julie, that was amazing," he said.

I smiled. I was a stud. I had never questioned what kind of a man I would be if I *were* a man and now, without exaggeration, I had waltzed right into being a stud. Oh, most guys would be so jealous. Imagine working your whole life to attain this kind of sensation. Imagine having to get over all those male insecurities, and here I was with my giant cock and what was more impressive was that I knew how to use it. I just knew, instinctively. It made me want to fuck absolutely everyone. I went over a list in my mind of various charming girls and boys. I thought of Kelly first. I thought of Hal. Oh, it was delightful.

"I feel so close to you right now, Julie," Simon whispered. "No woman has ever made me feel like you do before."

"Uh…" I didn't know how to respond. I was too tired and too spent to be mean to him about this. It was inappropriate. What did he mean? I vaguely paid attention. "Thanks, Simon." It seemed the only worthy comment.

"You're always saying not to be afraid, so I won't be afraid. There's something I have to tell you. I think I love you."

Whoa, whoa, whoa. Now this was something I absolutely was not ready for. It was a buzz killer. Here I'd thought we were having the most perfect time and he'd had to go and ruin it by talking about feelings. Feelings didn't enter into this, didn't he know that? Had he lost his mind? He was a good fuck. He had a gorgeous mouth. But love? I was confronted with the ultimate liability. I was too good a guy for my own good. I was too talented with my cock. That was what this was about.

"Oh, baby, you're just confused," I soothed him. He would back down. There were other cocks out there. None like mine, we both knew…but still. I felt too tired to engage with what he'd said, so it just irritated me. Nothing kills hotness like talking about feelings. At least, when you don't have them yourself.

I got up and started to get dressed.

"So that's it?" Simon asked.

"What do you mean?"

"Well…"

"Oh, you think that giving me a blow job entitles you to one in return? Is that how you think it works?"

"No. Not that… What I said before…"

"What? You have feelings for me? You want me? You want me to let you fuck me? Jeez, Simon, you're not one to speak your mind."

"I just opened my heart to you."

"Oh, come on. So you have a bit of a crush on me. So what?" I chose to downplay the whole thing. My buzz was shot. I felt a complete mental clarity, despite my still quivering cunt.

"It's not just a crush, Julie. I love you. I'm sure of it."

"Well, that's not possible."

"Of course it's possible."

"Fine. It's not reciprocated."

"Are you sure? I saw the way you looked at me before."

"When?"

"When I was kissing your dick."

"Kissing? I was gagging you with my cock. See? You and I are made up of different material, Simon. I like you, don't get me wrong," I said, and stopped myself from saying, 'I like your mouth'. "But, realistically, I don't think it's possible for you to love me when you don't even understand me."

"You don't know that."

"Oh, I think I do."

His obsequious nature was too much for me to handle. I loved the feeling of it when we were fucking, but not afterwards. It couldn't go on like this. He just wasn't challenging enough.

"Give me another chance," he pleaded, lying on the floor as I stood fully dressed and ready to leave the studio.

"Chance at what? You're not making sense."

"What I mean is… Don't fire me. Let me stay. Forget what I said. Don't worry about it. They're my feelings. It isn't your problem."

"You're right, Simon, it's not my problem. I'm a busy woman. I have many things and people to tend to, so don't expect me to pay you too much attention."

"Anything you wish, Julie. I'll do anything."

"Fine. Get dressed. I guess the fitting went well. It isn't at all too snug like you were afraid of. I think it's just right."

I handed Simon the limp harness for his finishing touches. "I'll pick this up in a few hours," I said, and he nodded in agreement.

I felt oddly guilty as I left his studio. Had I deceived him? Was it wrong of me to have been so predatory? Then I shook that thought from my head. What was wrong with it? He had wanted to suck my cock as badly as I'd wanted him to. If anything, he had deceived *me*. I'd thought it was just about the sex. I'd thought it was about my cock, my hardness, my irresistibility. Really, all along, it was about his feelings. But what did he expect would come of that? It made me mad to think of how presumptuous he had been. How utterly selfish. Those were his feelings that he was unloading on me. I didn't ask him for them. They were extremely ill-timed. I had just given of myself. How dare he disrupt my post-coital bliss with his inconvenient declarations? What on earth was I to do with that?

Oh, it made me angry. I decided that, while Hal was away, I would fire Simon. It didn't much matter whether or not they were having relations. If they were, Simon could come back for that purpose. Either way, I would need a new and better tailor. This was ridiculous. I had enough to see to already. I had a wedding to plan. At the very least, I concluded, I had a wedding to attend. I didn't need some passive aggressive barnacle on me. I didn't need his manipulative ways.

My mind was made up. I went to my room and took a nap. I needed to recover. I woke up with a distinct feeling, a hard-on. I needed to feel my harness up against me again. I was virile and ready to go. I wanted to fuck more than ever.

At four, as planned, Simon came to Strawberry Hill. When I walked into my room, he had his back to me, looking out of the window. He was stretching his neck as if he had been hunched over for quite a while. A beautiful black gown was lying on my chaise longue. I walked towards him, startled him, and he turned to me.

"I didn't see you come in," he muttered.

"What's this?" I headed for the dress immediately. It was lovely. Raw silk, with an opening down the back. Slightly darker silk laces created a corset effect. It was stunning.

"I made that for you."

"When?"

"I've been working on it for a while."

"It's beautiful."

"Try it on. Oh, and, about earlier, I apologise. It wasn't my place to say anything. Obviously nothing can happen between us. You're almost married and I... Well, I work for you...and your husband."

Ordinarily that kind of reasoning irritated me. Love has nothing to do with such shallow definitions of who we are and how we're able to relate to each other, but I didn't think telling him that would help.

"I'm glad you figured it out, Simon. It would be wrong for us to continue this." I was calm, collected and professional about it. I have always believed that diplomacy is one of the most important characteristics a person can develop. It shows refinement, manners and maturity. I was proud of myself for my conduct. I just wasn't proud of the fact that I secretly wanted to know what it felt like to penetrate Simon's ass with my cock. I suppose it was wrong of me to have those feelings and simultaneously let him believe that we were rigidly separated by titles.

I guess that is always the case when morality enters into the realm in which it does not belong. Sexuality, they say, is instinctual. I disagree. I think that with enough questioning and sincerity, one can become a finely tuned machine of innate sexual desires, but never without taking into account how that very sexuality has been taken from us time and again. And here was Simon taking another unnecessary precaution. I didn't have a moral issue with us fucking. Hal didn't, either. It was Simon who was incapable of detaching himself from reading a whole lot more into it. It was tragic. We could really have enjoyed each other. Maybe it was worth trying for. I was smitten with his pedantic attention to detail. He was the perfect tailor and could be the perfect lover. With that knowledge, I set out to enjoy his boyish charms. I wanted to at least have a little practice before unleashing my giant cock on Hal. I needed the training.

"Simon." I called him the following day. "I need you for a little project."

"Sure, Julie, when would you like to see me?"

"Two o'clock. Your studio," I said. It was that easy. And that difficult.

Chapter Thirteen

I wasn't entirely sure what I had in mind with Simon, except that I wanted to see him more, even though I understood it would most likely result in devastation. He didn't matter that much to me. That is one of those truthful declarations that good people would look down upon, but it was true. Still, he was the perfect boy toy, the ideal distraction from a wedding I was becoming increasingly anxious about.

"Hello, darling." I propped myself up on some pillows on Simon's single bed, which he kept in his studio. I had become quite fond of my sojourns into town to visit Simon. I was wearing a flirty chiffon scarf, which I tossed about me like a movie star. He was obviously taken aback. The poor guy. We were probably about the same age, but I felt older.

"Uh. Hello." He fumbled as he sat down on the simple wooden chair next to the bed. "I'm surprised to see you so soon or, rather, I'm surprised you wanted to see me so soon."

"Soon? Darling, you're the best tailor I know. How could I live without you?" I did my best to feign delicate mannerisms. My theatrical debut was over the top. "Simon, I need you to do something for me."

"And what might that be, Julie?"

"I need you to fuck me."

He coughed and turned scarlet. Then he smiled. Then he looked around, loosening his collar. This boy was awkward.

"Oh, come on, dear. Is this going to be a problem for you?"

"Um... Well... I told you I think I'm falling in love with you."

"Oh, that. Well, get over it."

"Julie, it's not something you just get over."

"Don't lecture me about love, Simon. This is professional. I want to know what the jade cock feels like. It's important to me. I trust you to do it right."

"Wait a minute. Fuck you with the jade cock?" He looked baffled.

"Yes. My cock. I want my cock."

He was puzzled. He shook his head and seemed insulted.

"Oh, don't sulk," I said. "I'll let you use your cock, too. It's just that I'm obsessed with my dick and I want to know what it feels like before I use it on Hal."

"What's wrong with you? Do you not have a heart? Or have you just never used it?"

"Broaden your mind, dear boy." I pulled my fingers through my hair. "What good is your love for me if you can't even bring yourself to fuck me?"

"You really are quite a woman, Julie. Does Hal know you're here?"

"Of course. But the cock is a surprise."

"How thoughtful."

"Simon, I need you. I have to get good first. It's like anything else, I suppose. Anyway, I'm offering you an opportunity, but if you want to turn it down..."

Was it cruel to toy so with him? Most definitely. Could I help myself? Absolutely not.

"I'm not going to turn it down." He reached out to me and took my hand in his. I toyed with the fantasy of context for a moment. What would it be like to live a life with him, somewhere outside this reality? Considering that Hal was one of his biggest clients, we were both utterly reliant on the same source for our livelihoods. Yet my mind wandered. I imagined Simon in a remote cabin, reading by a fireplace, chopping wood occasionally. I imagined him with a full collection of classical music. I imagined him keeping chickens, making omelettes for me in the mornings. It was quaint, eccentric. It wasn't what I wanted, of course, but the fantasy was compelling.

"Kiss me, darling." I was on my back on his bed and pulled him onto me. It was seductive. If I had been him, I also would not have resisted.

I could feel his cock harden against me. I loved it. The cosiness of his space added to my affections. He kissed my neck and ran his lips lightly over my ears, which sent shivers down my spine. I felt the tingle in my cunt and he reached around me with both arms. It felt so good. Unlike all of our other interactions, this time, he was on top of me, in control—or at least, in my mind I could will it that way. Part of what attracted me to Simon was his overt attraction to me. His jubilation over my mere presence was flattering. I love attention. I always have and there was something about the transference that Simon gave me. It was almost as though he gave me attention at the cost of leaving any for himself.

It felt to me as though Simon was malleable. It felt as if I could train him to do anything I wanted. What I wanted at that moment was more than his boyish charms. I wanted to feel manly hands on me, to be whisked away the way Timothy had on the yacht — the kind of feeling that allowed me to be completely feminine and feel small in his arms, and even smaller intertwined with his body.

It was difficult with Simon. Even if he was able to summon that state of mind, which was debatable, our bodies were incapable of reflecting what our minds expressed. He wasn't much bigger than my five-and-a-half foot frame. He was a little broader — that was natural — but he didn't exude masculinity, as they say. Of course, as I have come to understand it, masculinity means many different things and is, at best, a relative term. That Simon should want to suck my cock as opposed to me sucking his seemed perfectly natural and did not indicate any less of a degree of masculinity in him. If anything, I felt that he was a real man, capable of understanding femininity in a less than structured and conventional way. That was what it took, perhaps. That was also what I expected from Hal when I finally got to him.

But for now the challenge seemed to lie within me. It was my relationship with my cock that mattered more than either Simon's or Hal's relationship with it. I wondered if that was a self-centred thought, but concluded there was only one natural way to approach the subject. I would have to experiment. I would have to learn what felt good and, for this, Simon would be much more useful than Hal — with Hal, the stakes were higher.

I guess that is the thing with familiarity. Once a love relationship is established, one feels intimidated to try new things, to experiment, for fear, perhaps, that one's love might think it a sign of disloyalty or disrespect. One might assume that a new leaf — a dangerous leaf — has been turned over. I was thankful it would all be quite new with Hal. We had a sexual history, but it was really only vicarious. It had been profound and I needed the profundity to continue, and that was why I needed a practice run at it. That and, of course, there was the matter that Simon's lips were on my neck and I was breathing heavily beneath him.

I rolled out from beneath him, flipped him onto his side and lay beside him for a while, watching him look at me. His attention made me feel adored. He was like a poet, studying me, trying to extrapolate just the right line from the situation we shared. He caressed my face with his gentle fingers. I could almost hear him falling in love with me. I could feel him take steps further and further towards the inevitable heartache I would cause him. Sure, I could choose to feel bad about it, but he was doing it to himself.

I wanted to warn him, wanted to tell him I was not what he projected onto me. He certainly wasn't the first man to go down the road he was on. I think that every sexually free woman invites her share of disdain for doing what I was doing with Simon. Knowing that made me appreciate him even more. He wasn't the only poet between us. He brought something out in me, something romantic and wonderful.

I loosened his shirt and removed it. I tossed it on the floor, which riled him up to no end. His studio was spotless. I was quite convinced that he neatly folded every article of clothing he had worn that day before putting it to laundry. I really had fun with Simon. Just because I knew how much it irked him, I did the same with his pants—I simply tossed them on the floor, not even in a pile, just wild and willy-nilly. Poor, poor Simon.

Then I lay him on his back and straddled him. I was so wet and ready. I slowly pulled my black crew neck top up over my breasts, then up over my head. Even though my vision was blurred by the fabric, I could feel his eyes on me, could feel his stare penetrate even my bra. He seemed obsessed with my nakedness, seemed to savour every step that brought him closer.

So there we were, like two high school students with our pants still on and my bra still on and him ready to come. I let him take his time with me. He gently glided his fingers over my belly and around my side. No, this was not a man who knew what the hot spots were and went there immediately. Simon was really more of a novice, an impressionable traveller in foreign territory. And, after all the hands that had touched me with the arrogance of their seeming knowledge of women's bodies, Simon was a refreshing change. I let him explore my midriff with open palms. I let him ogle my black lace bra. I could feel his response to it. For a tailor, I was a little shocked that he was so in awe and yet, I thought, what a disappointment it must be to work with the materials on a daily basis, only to end up with empty garments. Yes, it definitely was not the garment he was taking an interest in.

"Unhook it," I whispered, leaning down over him to give him access. My long hair landed on his face, causing him to flinch a little. I tickled his nose with my hair.

"Really?" he asked, innocent as a young boy. "Are you sure?"

I nodded. I stayed down close to his face, resting against his chest. His hands ran sensually over my back.

"Your skin is so soft," he said. "Sorry. I know that's a cliché. You must hear that all the time. Not all the time. I'm sorry. You know what I mean."

"Relax, Simon. Just relax and take off my bra and enjoy my skin, okay?"

"Yes, ma'am. I mean, Julie."

I wanted to roll my eyes at him but found myself smiling instead. There was something about him that was so sweet and docile, it made me feel special. I felt as if I were one of the Seven Wonders of the World, not because he'd said so but because of what he hadn't said. I'm sure if I had asked him to, he would have told me how he felt. But it was nice to let myself experience his utter admiration.

Simon did as I instructed. I felt his fingers unhook the tiny clasp on my black lace bra. I kissed his neck and, as if I were unveiling a masterpiece for the first time, I arched my back and came back to the upright seated position. I was still straddled over him, this time giving him the perfect vantage point for my God-given assets.

I took his hands, cupped each one and slowly brought them up to my breasts. My nipples became immediately hard when he touched them with the relatively rough skin of his soft hands. He was gentle at first, then I squeezed his fingers around my nipples and moaned in pleasure.

Something about the experience made me change my mind. In the back of my head, I had thought I wanted to fuck Simon's ass. I did. But I also wanted him to fuck me. I wanted his cock inside me, much to my own surprise. I crouched down, slid past his knees in my seated position and prised his briefs from him. Even his cock suggested youth. I took it in my mouth and almost immediately his eyes rolled back into his head and his fists tightened. I wondered if Simon was thinking of baseball or England or his grandmother to ward off an embarrassing moment. He was solid in my mouth and I rhythmically pumped up and down, gripping him firmly with my lips. Suddenly, he pulled back.

"What's the matter?" I asked in my quiet, husky way. I was deviously curious.

"It's just that... I was about to... I can't handle... Oh, Julie, you're just so beautiful."

"Is it really my beauty that's overwhelming? Why don't you just go ahead and come if you want to? There will be plenty of opportunity for more later."

"I want it to be good...for you. I want to last."

"Why last when you can come again and again? This is something I'll never understand about the male psyche. Look at me. When I want to come, I come. I know I'll be able to come again."

"But what about you? I mean isn't it important for me to last for just that reason, to make you come?"

Simon was refreshingly sweet.

"There are plenty of things you can do for me without your cock if it's a matter of you wanting a respite."

"Really?"

"I have big plans for you this afternoon. Much bigger than your cock alone could even hope to handle."

"Oh, yeah?"

I kissed him. Then I repositioned myself at his cock and took him into my mouth again. His erection grew with my bobbing movements and soon I found the most enjoyable rhythm. I loved the feeling of having him in my mouth and, perhaps even more so, I loved the thought of being a mind-blowing experience for him. I fondled his balls as I gently sucked on his cock, pulling it farther and farther into my mouth. I found his ass with a finger and, with a small amount of pressure, he opened up to me and I gingerly eased my way inside him. I wriggled around a bit, seductively calling on his inner libertine. His moans grew louder and louder, then I felt the pulsating thrust of his ejaculation as he emitted a giant cry of relief. His hot liquid pumped through his body like the most virile blood and what sprang forth was the most delicious concoction of warmth. I took it all in my mouth and swallowed. This, to him, must have been utterly unthinkable because he looked at me with disbelief. He became limp soon after and was almost unable to speak. Nothing he mumbled made sense, so I giggled. There was something so sincere and juvenile about it.

I was almost tempted to let the experience stop there—it had been perfect. It was perfect for him, I was sure. But I was a woman with needs of my own. I had my motivations for being there, and pleasing Simon, while fun, was not part of my overall agenda.

I got up from the bed, unzipped my jeans and placed them neatly with my top, over the back of his chair. I took my bra from beside him on the bed and placed it neatly over my pants. Simon was resting his head on his folded arms, watching me and glancing at the pile on the floor. He smiled calmly, as though he finally grasped the game I'd been playing with him. I bent down, removed my panties and folded them. Teasing him was deeply arousing. Then I stepped on his clothes on my way back onto the bed and knelt beside him.

I reached my hand out for his, which he gave me without hesitation. I placed his fingers at the opening of my cunt to let him feel my wetness. His cock twitched a little and promptly, as though inconsistent with his beliefs about himself, he was erect again.

"Oh, my God. Oh, my God..." he whispered. I was flattered by his lack of pretence. He was unlike other men. He was more than willing to acknowledge his gratitude. His face gave him away completely.

I reached into my bag, which I'd handily situated at the side of the bed, and pulled out my jade dildo. I handed it to him. Then I seated myself on his chest and sat there with my wetness teasing him. We stared at each other intently for what seemed like a long time. It felt as if I were eating him with my eyes. I wanted to feel him inside me, such an eager young man, and I wanted to feel my own cock because it held such mystery to me. I straddled his face, guiding his awaiting tongue to my cunt. He grabbed on to my hips and pulled me against his lips, pushing his tongue farther inside as he pulled my pelvis towards his. I fondled my cock and passed it to Simon.

"Put my cock in me," I ordered.

The jade felt smooth and grand as it pressed against my opening. I engulfed it greedily and let him push it into me. It was a strange feeling—like fucking myself, in a way—and I loved it. He was in awe as well. I wondered if it evoked feelings of jealousy in him. It must have. To be upstaged by my cock could not possibly be good for his ego, and yet I wanted him to understand that sex was not about the goal of climaxing, and that it didn't end with male ejaculation. For a woman like me, sex could go on and on for a long time, and I was not dependent on his hardness even though he was proffering it again. I gyrated a bit and let him push and pull as I pinched my own nipples high above him. I turned around briefly and glanced at his massive erection. I had done a smart thing by letting him come once first.

I took my cock out and guided it to his mouth. He opened gleefully and licked my juices from it. I ran it along his lips, and then traced the length of my pussy with it before calmly, quietly and methodically backing onto it with my ass. This had been a fantasy for a long time but I had not acted on it. I'd wanted to know what my cock felt like and it exceeded my wildest expectations. I guided his hand to the dildo so that he could hold it for me as I moved backwards onto it. Once it was inside my ass, I felt myself open up to it. He gave it a nudge and it went deeper. I had to breathe slowly and fixate on the sensation of being fucked there for the first time. Simon toyed with me, pulling the dildo out and pushing it back in. He moaned as though he were fucking my ass with his own cock. The intensity between us was surprising and I wanted more. Once Simon thrust it deep inside, the jade cock stayed firmly planted in my ass. It had been so beautifully and carefully crafted, with a rim around the shaft. It stayed in place all by itself.

I shifted backwards towards Simon's cock. He was eagerly anticipating my arrival. I reached into my bag, pulled out a condom and tore the package open, again tossing the wrapper as far as I could into a corner, so that he would have to look for it to dispose of it properly as soon as he had his strength back.

His hardness amazed me. His cock was so much harder than when I'd had it in my mouth, and I eased myself onto him with slight trepidation. Two cocks at one time was a fantasy I had not expected to turn into reality. I had done many things in the past few months, but this was a first. He guided me slowly onto him with gentle hands, and stared at my pussy as I hovered above him. He held his cock with his right hand and slid it into my cunt with precision. He moaned and gave a thrust with his hips so that the tip of his cock entered my pussy. I appreciated the slowness of his movements. He showed remarkable restraint. I had to practice patience as well as I lowered myself onto his cock ever so gently. There was pain but I embraced it. It was the good kind.

My mind marvelled at the sensation of being completely filled up. I could feel the two cocks inside me, stretching me. I sighed with bliss as I felt the union take place and pushed myself farther and farther onto him. In terms of intensity, this was beyond anything I had ever imagined. I started convulsing and steered straight towards a massive orgasm brought on, I thought, by my mind more than my body. It was an out-of-body experience. I saw myself stretched, about to reach a threshold of pain that would push me beyond pleasure. I soared on that fine line into the sweet abyss of orgasm. My muscles contracted around Simon's cock as well as my own and it felt as though I was bursting. The rapture of it was almost frightening.

It took me by surprise that this position and these feelings had made me come so quickly. It couldn't be the same as having two men take me at once. This feeling hinged on my sexual ego, and I loved my cock. Double penetration had always been a fantasy of mine but I'd always felt as if the reality would be disappointing. The men would really have to control themselves, and I also knew that the kind of orgasm I'd like to achieve through double penetration would be so huge that I'd need the freedom to succumb to it fully, without the pressure of continued fucking. Simon was the perfect penetration partner. His eager cock filled my cunt and left me free to admire the feeling of my own cock. No longer having to imagine what it felt like satisfied not only my curiosity but also catapulted me into a self-love I hadn't encountered before. I felt all of our movements — my convulsions and his adjustments — with acuteness and the largesse of my fantasy being actualised made me come again.

Simon looked as if his head were about to explode, as if he couldn't even fathom what was happening. I writhed, moaned and clung to him so hard I left dark red marks all over his shoulders. He watched me with wide eyes and the intensity of a spectator at an exorcism. My ass muscles contracted ferociously around my glorious cock. Meanwhile, my clit rubbed against the shaft of Simon's hard dick and the combination of my self-sodomy and his gentle lovemaking attempt created a perfect springboard for a deluge of fluids to spill forth from inside me. Just as the waterfall orgasm Sam had given me had taken me by surprise and forced me to rethink everything I knew about sex, this simultaneous orgasm in both my cunt and my ass not only lasted forever, but I knew it's repercussions would be that I'd upped my own ante. I panted and moaned and savoured every second of pleasure.

I was thrilled. I don't remember a time I had felt more alive. Simon was the perfect foundation and the perfect support. He lay underneath me, adoring my orgasm and sharing it as much as I would have, were our positions reversed. I barely even noticed that he had also come. I hadn't felt it during my own explosive orgasm but I could sense that he had become flaccid. I felt the gentle throbbing of his cock, still twitching from having expunged its semen. I could feel the warmth of it through the condom. He held onto my waist as we both fell, stunned, to his mattress for a blissful rest.

After a moment of enjoying Simon's strokes through my hair and his delicate touch, I dismissed myself and went home. The following morning, I made another appointment for Simon's professional services.

"I need you to procure a few more items for me, darling," I told him on the phone, twirling my hair between my fingers.

"Anything."

"I was hoping you would say that. I need a hand-carved ivory cock. Something…oh, worthy of me." I batted my lashes and flipped my hair over my shoulder, even though he couldn't see me.

"Nothing but the best, then."

"I'm glad we see eye to eye on this."

"So the jade wasn't to your liking?"

"The jade was grand. It's just that a girl needs variety."

"I'm sure I can oblige. Anything else?"

"Well, the harness is beautiful. I'll need some wrist restraints and also…" I trailed off for a moment, thinking about implements. "I haven't made up my mind about everything I need but you can take the artistic licence to be creative," I said.

After I put down the phone, I lay on my bed, in my room. I massaged my feet and thought about what I had done. Simon undoubtedly thought that the reason I wanted his opinion was that he was somehow to partake in the goods. He probably thought that all of my collectibles would work to his advantage. Well, there is grave error in assumption. If he didn't already know that, he was about to learn.

In a way, I felt like a magician learning new tricks. In the ordinary and mundane world, where everyone behaves according to a code of conduct that was built on centuries of codes of conduct, behaviour measures value. Under ordinary circumstances, I'd be a bitch to trick poor Simon into doing his best work for me by making him think that he was actually working for himself. But that would be irrational and illogical. Not only would I get to provide him with an important lesson about meeting my needs, I would also get to show him that he must learn to suppress his own needs in favour of mine. Men are so predictable. Give them an inkling of corporeal reward and they fall all over themselves trying to reach some kind of imagined finish line.

Even Simon. Simon, the delicate, gentle Simon. The virgin, I thought. I hoped to teach Simon the value of selfishness and sexuality. It would have pleased me to see him take charge with me, but I didn't expect it. It's not the kind of quality that can be taught. And the benefit would be to him, not to me. I chose to accept the way he passively embraced my agenda in the hopes of appeasing me and earning more access to me.

Sometimes I wished I knew what it was like to be taken. I wished that a man would take me the way I'd just taken Simon. Timothy had been deliciously forceful but I craved to experience a man who was capable of choreographing something so incredible that my mind would have to surrender completely. So far, I had only seen evidence of a ubiquitous condition amongst men, a collective unspoken pact between them that they'd give me what I asked for. Perhaps it was me. Maybe this was what I brought out in men. I knew I had a special gift, one I could not define. I wasn't sure if it was as simple as flirtation or intimidation or any such quality. I was absolutely positive it had nothing to do with looks. In that department, I wasn't as blessed, relative to how they treated me. I was all right. I did okay, but I wasn't like the women I saw. I wasn't as graceful as Francine Jean. I didn't have Kelly's or Carla's physique. I wasn't a trophy wife. I packed a few more pounds than necessary. Somehow, it had never been about that. Everyone had always told me I was beautiful, then said that it was my personality. What did that mean?

Chapter Fourteen

I picked up my brush and sat by my vanity to smooth my hair. After Simon, I felt a great need to spend time alone. I think I needed to make sense of all of the things I'd engaged myself with, and that can really only be done in solitude. Looking at my face in the mirror, I noticed how I had changed. My face was different now than I remembered it being the last time I had taken a good look. I had been in Virginia for the last couple of months. I had met Hal three weeks prior to leaving San Francisco. I was lucky it had all worked out like this.

Lucky. What did that mean?

Other wives-to-be would have been busy in the throes of love with the man they had agreed to marry. We hadn't even scaled the three-month mark. But it wasn't like that with Hal. I was off having a consensual adulterous affair with my tailor—his tailor. And he was with whomever in Atlanta, Georgia, on a supposed business trip—well, what did I know of his trips? What did I know of whom he chose to be with?

I remember sitting there at my vanity and thinking about how my logic had changed. Even a few months earlier — just before meeting Hal — I would have thought that considering myself lucky in this situation would have everything to do with the huge mansion I was in and the giant ring on my finger, and a rich man's affirmation that I would never have to worry about money again. In my dreams, that had been some kind of fantasy ideal. I would have sacrificed ordinary permutations of happiness in order to achieve it. I would have been fine with a man who was less than perfect, a man who was uncaring or adulterous, because I would have seen the whole enterprise as a job. I would have looked at my duties as being a public persona.

I'd thought that was what Hal wanted me for. I had been quite convinced of it when he'd embraced his attraction to men. I had been sure of it the whole way here with Timothy and I was still sure of it at that point, with him being away — that he was out exercising his virility with the lads of the land. What surprised me, utterly threw me for a loop, was that I felt lucky on a personal account. How many people can say that? Hal was a wonderful man. He had been gentle and compassionate from the first time we'd met. But what really got to me, in a way that I had not imagined, was his complexity. I was smitten with his insecurities.

I'd always found men's insecurities to be heinous. From Tommy to that idiot college boy who'd first come to visit me at Carla's, to all of my drivers, to almost all the men I'd ever known. Especially, I thought, men who'd grown up wealthy, like Hal. They had an air. They had a claim to things. Then they felt bad about some other component of their lives and it made me sick, because they didn't even know what work was. They didn't understand what it meant to feel inferior to a whole class of people, and they had no idea what it was like to grow up working with both your parents, trying to make a living off the land. I'd never expected anyone to understand what my childhood meant to me. It was, after all, my childhood, not theirs. But some men were so inclined to ignore the distinct possibility that I used to have a life before they came along, that I did, in fact, function as an entirely independent mind and body and that I had drawn my own conclusions about my power and abilities.

Why did I suddenly feel understood by Hal? Perhaps it wasn't the kind of understanding wrought by similar experience, but more a respect wrought by struggle for freedom from conventional logic. Hal and I hadn't had sex by conventional standards, but I felt a solidarity, an intimacy with him that was greater than any I had known with a man before. So, indeed, I was lucky.

And I had a week left until he came back from Georgia and married me in our verdant Southern garden under the autumn sun, for the whole world to see. I had arrived. I had achieved more than I had hoped to and, although my satisfaction was something I'd have to keep private, I was intent on welcoming him with a physical experience that could satisfy both of us. And since it was entirely optional on my part — Hal being content to merely have me at his side — I felt like our union would be sanctified and honest and pious and beautiful. I wanted to give him the greatest pleasure he'd ever known.

To most men, that would mean intense orgasms followed by boosts to the ego. That wasn't Hal. I couldn't imagine us in the missionary position. I couldn't imagine what it would be like to sit on his cock. I couldn't even imagine him ejaculating the way most men do. It would be unique with us. Entirely unique. I hoped my cock would do him justice. I hoped that it would be what he wanted, even if he had never imagined it. I was determined to take him by storm, to provide for him more than mere companionship and paperwork.

It was a strange order of happenings. We'd met, got engaged in a superficial relationship, moved in together, were about to get married...then I realised I was in love with him. That was the genesis of my deciding to woo him.

* * * *

"Your new cock is here," Simon announced on the phone a few days later.

"I'll come by for a fitting," I told him. "Have you tailored the second harness?"

"I think everything is perfect."

"I knew it would be."

* * * *

I sipped my morning coffee and browsed the local paper.

Hal, who had come home late the night before, stumbled into the dining room with his robe loosely covering him. He poured tea from his antique porcelain pot into his teacup, added a sugar cube and stirred. Lynette, his assistant, dropped the usual pile of mail in front of him and he proceeded to slice each envelope open with his silver opener.

It was our usual morning routine, which I had become accustomed to and loved. I cherished our silent mornings — we were comfortable around each other and didn't need to talk.

Hal put his head down, rested his forehead on his index finger.

"What's the matter?" I asked.

"Nothing. Well, not nothing. Timothy's coming to the wedding...with his wife."

"Oh, dear." I buttered my croissant.

"Yeah. What are we going to do with them?" He was clearly concerned.

"Lie."

"I meant activity-wise."

"So did I."

"Oh, you're so clever." He smiled. Then he sighed. "She's a nightmare."

"To say the least."

"It makes me tired just thinking about her — all those questions. She's going to want to know all the details leading up to the wedding, all the details about our life together."

"Well, so what?"

"So, her brother is one of the high-ups at immigration."

"Well, shouldn't that work in your favour?"

"*Should* would be the operative word. Francine Jean is... Well, she's known to be mean and vindictive, and should she ever suspect anything about Timothy..."

"She won't."

"How can you be so certain?"

"Because she's the kind of woman who's so deeply repressed that even if she had an inclination towards the thought, any kind of unbridled passion is repugnant to her and she'd dismiss it instantly. She'd go back to her gardening or embroidery or gossip or whatever she passes the time with," I assured him.

Whether I was right or wrong seemed irrelevant. There was no use in worrying about it. It was mere speculation and fear on Hal's part.

The manor was a frenzy of activity in the days leading up to the wedding ceremony. I was nervous and excited, like a debutante awaiting the ball. It was surreal for me, a reality I'd never imagined. And I did everything I could to look and fit the part. I hired aestheticians to come to the house. I was waxed and manicured and pedicured and tweezed and dyed and painted and powdered and moisturised and massaged for days. It got to the point where I almost became tired of it. Almost. But not quite.

The day before the wedding, our guests started to trickle in. Mostly, they were composed of Hal's compatriots, business allies and old friends. None of his family members from England came. I'd only ever told Hal that my family had all been killed in a horrible accident. Being estranged from them carries too much of a stigma. I would have no guests at the wedding. I'd thought about inviting Kelly, but she seemed a world away. Hal's guests would have found Sam's attendance inappropriate. I would have liked it. But at least Timothy would be there. Simon, who had been invited, had made up a convenient story about having to be out of town.

On the morning of the big day, I met with my hair stylist and makeup artist and otherwise spent the morning preparing myself. It was a dream wedding, small and intimate, proper and stylish. The wedding planner had transformed a part of the estate and decorated the gazebo with dreamy white lace, dozens of white chairs, white roses and white lilies. The colour scheme couldn't have been more ironic, as I was hardly pure. Although I supposed that the white was appropriate for Hal and I.

As I walked down the aisle, I felt confident and happy. Hal was waiting for me at the altar. The ceremony was courteously brief and not overly sentimental. Our guests hobnobbed around the afternoon tea affair. Our cake was brilliant—a stunning three-tiered white cake with Italian meringue butter cream, topped with more lilies and roses. Everything was pretty and frilly and the ladies in attendance were ecstatic about pointing out the details to each other.

Meanwhile, I was ecstatically thinking about my wedding night. I was so anxious to give Hal my wedding gift. I desperately wanted to change out of the white, designer dress and into my custom leather harness.

But playing along with the high society niceties had its rewards as well. Hal dipped me during our song as we danced in front of our guests. An elderly lady in a wheelchair, accompanied by a nurse, sat in the far corner and said nothing to any of the guests. Hal told me later that she was his aunt Myrtle, the mysterious benefactor, and that she approved of me.

* * * *

My fateful night had finally arrived. After dinner, our guests left slowly, dawdling back to their rooms to pack their belongings and idly calling their chauffeurs. By the time they'd all made their exits of grandeur, Hal and I were both a bit peckish. Luckily, I had already arranged that the kitchen send a tray of chocolate-dipped strawberries, a bowl of whipped cream, some savoury snacks, some champagne and a jug of refreshing lemon iced tea. Preparations make the occasion, I've always believed. Hal was tipped off by the goings on. He was, as usual, taking a moment in his study when I came down to get him.

"There seems to be a fair bit going on tonight," he observed, though I had convinced myself that he wouldn't catch on.

"There certainly is."

"Are you having company?"

"On our wedding night? You could say that. I have a number of racy ideas up my sleeve tonight."

"Oh? Well, I'll stay out of your way then." He looked back down into his book. His glasses rested midway down his nose.

"You'll do no such thing, Hal."

He looked at me over the ridge of his glasses. I loved the way he could make eye contact with me, as if he were multi-tasking, like he was more distracted by me than by other preoccupations. There was an intensity about his eyes and a warmth that could not be beaten.

"Oh?" He closed his book but kept his thumb in the spine. "I thought you were preparing for a lover."

"I am, Hal. You."

He was perplexed.

"Come here, love." He patted his lap.

I came to his desk and sat on his thighs. I put my arms around his large neck and leaned my face into him. I loved the way he smelt. It made me feel both safe and excited.

"You know I love you, right?" he whispered.

"Mm-hmm."

"And you know you can have anyone you want, right?"

"Mm-hmm."

"So what are you doing this for?"

"What?"

He touched my hair, caressed my cheek, held me. "All of this. Why don't you save it for someone you'd rather choose?"

"I don't get it, Hal. What do you mean?"

"I mean I don't want you to feel any kind of obligation. You know I love you the way you are, and I know you love me the way I am, and..."

"Hal, I really love you the way you are," I said and kissed him softly. He pulled his face back ever so slightly.

"Honey..." I could feel his trepidation, his anxiety rising. He looked at me as if he thought I had forgotten all the rules and ideals we had so carefully established.

"I know what you're thinking, Hal. Don't. It's not like that. Just come upstairs to my room. I have a surprise for you."

"For me?"

"Yes. I've been planning it for a long time. I think you'll like it."

"Julie, you never cease to surprise me, with this, especially. Just when I thought I'd finally found a relationship I could understand..."

"What? Are you disappointed? You don't even know what the surprise is. Have a little faith. You know it's not going to be me in red lace. Relax."

Hal smiled his coy smile. I could tell that, underneath his nay-saying, he was sincerely flattered. It was a magic time. We were scaling uncharted territory together. It was a strange mixture of vicarious attraction, fascination and love.

I went back up to my room, pulled my harness on, opened my velvet-lined briefcase and examined my cocks. I had had Simon commission a specially-made carry-case for me that fit each cock perfectly. Simon had liked the idea as much as I did. There was something about having a kit, like a toolkit, that made me feel like more of a magician than a woman, which was exactly how I wanted to feel. If I was going to use props instead of my God-given gifts, I wanted them to be beautiful extensions of me. I wanted them to be as valuable as I was. I had spent thousands on my collection of cocks. I was sure then, and I'm still convinced now, that they are the finest collection this country has ever seen. And no one had seen them but me and Simon, their designers, crafters and carvers...and now Hal.

My ivory cock had a gemstone ring around the base of it. Amethysts embedded in gold, then meticulously ensconced in the ivory in an ornate Rococo-inspired design. The cock itself was slightly curved, so that it would have the appearance of a natural erection. I loved the details on it. It had a head with life-like veins and lines and the texture at the tip was smooth but skin-like to the touch. If not for the temperature and the paleness, it would have made any man an object of envy. I could warm it against my thighs and the pallor suited my own alabaster skin tone. The size was smaller than many of the men I had seen, but its shape was what made it so spectacular. My admiration of my own perfect cock gave me a mental hard-on I couldn't ignore. I was aching to feel myself grind against Hal. I wanted to fuck my husband more than anything I'd ever wanted.

The sensitive part of me kept reminding myself to slow down, that I had taken all of these steps in an effort to show Hal how much I loved him. And that was true. But, in addition to that awareness, I was more aroused than I could ever muster at the anticipation of being penetrated. Having a cock inside me was one thing. Getting to thrust myself into him would be quite another. And the best part was knowing that he favoured the sensation.

I rubbed my cock, admiring the sight of myself in the mirror. The harness held the cock perfectly in place and I could feel the strap underneath each time I moved. Never before had I been this wet, this anxious, this eager. I rubbed and rubbed, giving myself the most extraordinary hand job. I was almost about to come when I heard my door open and close. I quickly removed the cock from the harness so that I wouldn't give away the surprise. I stepped out from behind my Japanese screen, wrapping my silk belt around my black robe.

"What's all this?" Hal asked. He must have been referring to the many candles I had arranged all around my room. My bed was the centrepiece attraction. On it, I had laid out my softest linen and the silver tray with snacks from the kitchen. My bedside table held the water jug and glasses. The ambient lighting and my preparations all led Hal to the only natural conclusion he could come to.

"Um, Miss Julie, I'm not sure if I'm comfortable with all of this...attention." He became shy and mysterious, like prey. In my mind's eye, I saw him as a gentle lamb that I would have to lull into an uncanny calm in order to properly seduce.

"Champagne?" I asked.

"No, thanks," he answered.

I poured two glasses anyway. I wasn't about to listen to him. It was just his fear and discomfort talking. What did they know? Had any woman asked this of him before? I highly doubted it. His previous experiences and attempts at heterosexual unions had involved women whose main interests were family and reproduction, being the good girls that they probably were. I went with my assumption that being with me was an altogether different experience, one he knew nothing about. This would be like losing his virginity all over again.

"Here you are." I handed him the flute glass. We clinked our crystal together.

"To us," I said, "and to you for making me so happy."

"Do I really make you happy?" he asked.

"Oh, Hal, you can't even begin to understand."

"Because you've already made me happy, Julie."

"Quit talking about us in the past tense. We're here now. Let me draw you a bath."

"A bath?"

"Sure."

"Where is all of this coming from?"

"More importantly," I said, "you should be asking yourself, 'Where is this going?'"

I winked and walked slowly to my clawfoot tub in the adjacent room. The leather strap tucked underneath my cock, beneath my robe, toyed with my clitoris with each step I took. I indulged in the feeling. Knowing it was there, and that Hal did *not* know, was part of the immeasurable pleasure. I could not help myself. I stopped again at my full-length mirror just inside the bathroom and admired myself. I stroked my cock with the kind of pride I could only imagine a select few men capable of.

The slate tiles in my bathroom were warm—a renovation that Hal had made prior to my moving in. I enjoyed the luxury of it. I stood on the plush, off-white bath mat and ran the water. The porcelain tub was probably over a century old and in immaculate condition. My room had not been occupied for ages. I think it had served as a guest room ever since the house was built. I opened a luxurious and expensive jar of body wash crème. The sudsy lather emitted a savoury ginger fragrance throughout the room that was both masculine and appealing to my girlie senses. I was quite sure Hal would approve if I could get him to play along.

"Come on in, sweetheart," I called towards the other room.

Hal was hesitant…and rightly so. I wondered what it must have been like for him before me. What kinds of women had he tried to have an understanding with? Where had he met women? Certainly most debutantes would not have been appropriate matches for him. Yet he had probably, at some point, been rumoured to be amongst the best catches of the South. He was so charming and well mannered, rich beyond comprehension, had a beautiful and well-maintained home and was handsome. His parents being gone could be seen as favourable in the efforts to meet women, given what I'd overheard about meddling Southern mothers.

Hal's footsteps approached the bathroom. The anticipation was wonderful. He came in and immediately took a deep breath.

"It smells wonderful in here."

"For you," I said. "Get in. Relax."

He tossed his robe onto the antique oak chair and lowered himself into the steaming, frothy bath. It looked so inviting. I love the feeling of baths.

"Are you getting in with me?"

"Nope. I'm going to exfoliate my darling for him."

"What's gotten into you?"

"Can't I be nice and chivalrous without some kind of devious plan attached to it?"

"I don't know. Can you?" He chuckled.

I got out the ginger-scented scrub and a loofah. I pushed the oak chair over to the side of the tub and sponged his back for him. He sighed. The intoxicating aroma was enough to send me into sheer fantasy and utter relaxation. I loved the indulgence of it all. Wasn't I, at least in part, busy seducing myself? Wasn't that what seducing someone else was really all about? Hal's skin, like most middle-aged men's, was losing its elasticity. Like most men, he had been taught to ignore it, to ignore himself.

"Men are socialised to believe that soap is the only necessary step in the cleansing ritual," I commented.

"What else is there?"

"See?" I rolled my eyes.

"No, really, what else is there? What are you doing now?"

I added a dollop of scrub to the loofah and made circles on his back.

"Exfoliation. How does that gritty sensation feel?"

"Like sandpaper."

"Be serious, Hal," I kissed the back of his neck.

"It feels wonderful. What does this do?"

"Removes dead skin cells."

"Gross."

"Grosser to just ignore them, isn't it?"

"You know, I'm not a pansy. I don't need all this."

"Hal, no one is calling you a pansy, least of all me. I assure you, I need a real man. A manly man. There's nothing pansy about maintaining yourself, though."

"Really?"

"Of course. Where did you learn otherwise?"

"I don't know. I've just never met anyone who did this kind of thing."

"Pamper you?"

"Yeah."

"Well, you're worth it. I love doing it. I love you."

After his bath, I towelled him off and made him lie face down on my bed while I quietly retrieved my cock and put it in place. Back on the bed, I used a ginger massage oil and massaged Hal everywhere. I spent at least an hour just touching him, firmly and smoothly. I felt a lovely symbiosis between us — his sighing and my enjoyment colliding to create a godly effect.

"No one has ever touched me like you do, Julie. No one."

"I don't believe you."

"Well, it's true. I feel like you've paid attention to every part of me."

"Not *every* part of you." I smoothed my palms over his ass and let my index finger dangle just slightly above his asshole.

"Mmm," he uttered, to my surprise. Was I to take this as an affirmation? I seemed to have gained his trust.

"I'm the one who should be saying, 'Mmm'. You're like my very own tasty roast. Marinated, tenderised. I want to sink my teeth into you."

"Why, Miss Julie!" He feigned surprise and disdain with an exaggerated Southern accent.

"Why, Mr Hal Broughton, whatever is the matter with you that you should choose such a perverse woman to be your wife?" I feigned my version of the accent right back.

He rolled onto his side, smiled at me and held out his hand. I put my hand in his and he brought the back of my hand to his lips and glossed over it with his mouth. "How did I manage to get this lucky?" He looked into my eyes. It was a powerful moment, a conventionally sweet moment, the kind of moment that women dream up in fantasies of gentlemen. It was the precise feeling that I needed to manipulate and change.

"Oh, Hal. You have no idea how lucky you really are," I said, then I pulled his hand, which was still attached to mine, down to my crotch and let his fingers feel my bulge. His eyes widened and his previously relaxed body became immediately attentive.

He giggled nervously. "What's this?"

He opened my robe just enough to reveal the first hint of my ivory cock. I smiled. Our eyes transmitted the electricity between us as his brain tried to process all the details of this magnificent day.

"Is this my surprise?"

I nodded.

"You can say no, Hal, but there is one fantasy that I'd really like to live out with you."

"And what might that be?"

"Don't play innocent with me, darling." I bent down and kissed his neck, then kept kissing him down the length of his spine. He moaned and sighed and stretched his arm back around himself to touch the length of my leg. I had done the perfect thing by forcing him to relax. I had taken the pressure off. I was confident and, above all, I was aroused beyond my wildest dreams.

Hal was his own reward. What Hal and I shared was beyond what I had shared with anyone before. I kneaded his ass cheeks with my fingers, eyeing my ruby ring as it sparkled in the warm candlelight. This was more than the dirty scenario I had envisioned. This was more profound than any sexual act I had had the pleasure of taking part in.

I dipped my finger into my vial of unscented oil. Hal's cheeks parted easily and I found myself at the rim of his pleasure hole immediately. I could have taken it slow but, as though by invitation, my finger slipped into him with ease. He moaned and his muscles contracted lovingly around my digit as I found my way deeper and deeper. He buried his face in the pillows on my bed and his moans became muffled.

Slowly and smoothly, I took my finger back. I asked him to turn over and lie on his side. I knelt in front of him and yanked gently on his hair, beckoning for him to intuit that I wanted a little oral gratification. My ivory cock insisted on feeling the warmth of his mouth.

The site of his mouth engulfing me was delicious. I could not have asked for a better setting or time. Everything about that moment was quite perfect, especially the confidence I gained that he was open to experiencing me in this way.

He closed his eyes as his mouth followed the shaft of my cock right down to the rim. I could tell that he was really applying himself to the task. I tweaked my own nipples in the private moment of his blindness to me. I felt so full of life and so eager to provide him with the pleasure of the truly refined. He tried to take all of my cock into his mouth and almost gagged at the fullness of my endowed wonder. I marvelled at the sight and adored everything about him. I petted his shoulders gently as he thrust his mouth onto my cock and fondled it with his tongue.

It was, not surprisingly, extremely intimate. I was preparing to take my husband in a position that a lot of men consider very vulnerable. I was so proud of him for overcoming his fears and for accepting what I wanted to give him. I moaned and tilted my head back in ecstasy. The evidence that I was enjoying myself inspired him. He opened his eyes and looked at me with desire. We were kindred.

"You're amazing," he told me and I felt not only adored, but sexy beyond belief. His acceptance and fondness for me mattered more than any piece of paper we had between us. I wanted to give him so much more than that.

"You don't even know yet, my dear." I winked. "Lie down."

"What?" He resorted to his innocent persona again.

"You heard me," I said. The fact that he needed me to be a little forceful with him was flattering to me. I didn't want to feel like a man with my cock. I just wanted to feel like a very powerful woman. A woman gifted with an endowment that would make even the most secure man jealous. That was how I had wanted to feel, and that was exactly how I felt.

"What are you going to do?"

"Nothing you won't enjoy. Now, enough with these questions. I want you to trust me. You do trust me, don't you, my sweet?"

"I think so," he said.

"You think so? You're in a pretty compromising situation for a guy who just *thinks* he can trust his partner."

"I trust you."

"That's better," I confirmed. "Well, if you really trust me, then relax."

I held on to his broad shoulders as I climbed on top of him, seating myself on the padding of his thighs. I admired the sight of my cock from my vantage point so much that it was no stretch for me to imagine coming on him, releasing some of my tension in a fluid form. I wanted to give him an orgasm first, though, before I gave one to myself.

I pressed my ivory member slowly against his oil-soaked anus. He moaned quietly, indicating a slight hesitation. Thankfully, I had enough confidence for both of us. I pushed ever so slightly against him and his trepidation seemed to dissipate. I got off him gently and manoeuvred him to make room for some pillows beneath his pelvis. He adjusted himself and spread his legs to make room for me. I positioned myself behind him and started stroking the contours of his hole with the tip of my cock. I circled his anus again with my cock and let the tip of it enter him. He welcomed the head of my cock. Watching myself slide into him gave me enormous satisfaction. I couldn't wait to be all the way inside him. I pushed more.

"Slowly," he cried.

I held back a little, but it was hard. I was anxious and it made me more forceful than I might ordinarily have been. I had waited for months for this moment. I was on top of the world. With just a few more pulsating hip motions on my part, I ploughed my erection into his waiting ass. He cried out with pleasure and wiped at the beads of sweat that poured down his forehead.

"Harder," he pleaded.

"I knew you would love this," I whispered as I held myself tightly against his back.

"Oh, I love this."

"What do you love?"

"This," he said.

"What, exactly? I want to hear you say it."

"I love this feeling," he offered.

"Be more specific."

He became very silent. Yes, this was awkward. And I was going to force him to deal with it. I wanted him to accept us for everything we were. I wanted us to be together, not just in body but linguistically, as well. I knew this was hard for him. Much harder, even, than having his ass fucked.

"I love your cock," he finally muttered.

"What was that? I didn't hear you."

"Don't tease me…"

"Then be louder," I ordered.

"I love your cock, Julie. I love your cock in my ass! Fuck me."

"That's it, my sweet. Just tell me what I want to hear and I'll give you want you want from me."

"Give it to me, Julie. Really give it to me. I want it hard. I want you to fuck me hard."

"That's it, baby. You tell me."

We were in bliss together. I loved his words cheering me on like that. I penetrated him deeper and deeper as a pool of sweat developed between our naked bodies. I had never felt that close to someone before. I had never felt that level of ecstasy. It was as if I had tapped into an alter-ego, only to realise that I had become myself. It was one of the most profound moments of self-realisation of my sexual life.

With a growing force inside me and the feeling that Hal was nearing his breaking point, I fucked him as hard as I could. My hair had fallen all about and was messily in my face as I pounded into him. I reached around his neck and held him almost in a headlock grip. I had released an animal inside myself that had been in hibernation my whole life. In that moment, I could not have stopped fucking Hal. I was out of control. And he loved it. His well-lubed ass pleaded for more, just as he pleaded for more with his mouth. I soaked up his words like my skin would soak up suntan lotion at the beach.

His breathing quickened and his pulse raced through his body. I could tell that he would not be able to control himself much longer. He let out a furiously strained moan and bucked up against me. I held onto him as if I were riding a horse and we were galloping through an open field. It was intense and my thoughts turned momentarily from my own experience. I became distracted by the loudness of Hal's moans and his hyperbolic struggling. He was like a fish in a net gasping for survival as he reached the climax of what he could handle. In spite of all my efforts to make this experience about him, my harness had been rubbing up against my clit. It had given me a whole new sensation. I became restless and unable to hold back my orgasm.

As he started to come and yelled and gripped at the blanket beneath us, I felt the familiar sensation of release come over me. Unfamiliar, however, was the way in which it happened. It felt as if I were coming through my cock. I felt as though I was ejaculating, just as I'd done with Sam, but that I was doing it on my own. That I was releasing this viscous liquid into my lover like a fertile male was a thought I could not resist. I did not resist anything. I just gave and gave and gave.

We sank into a heap on the bed in the aftermath. My cock came slowly out of him and made a final popping noise when released from his grip. We were sweaty and spent and I was completely in love. It was the most exhilarated exhaustion I'd ever felt. I savoured it like honey.

Hal filled both our glasses with cold water and we gulped thirstily at them. His usually rosy cheeks were an even more flushed scarlet hue and we collapsed on our backs, side by side.

I held my hand up, straightening my arm in the air to admire my ring. He raised his hand to meet mine and stroked it casually.

"Am I a good wife?"

"The best."

We looked at each other, still breathing heavily, and smiled at the serenity of the situation. There is a kind of gratitude I've felt for all lovers who provide me with an incredible orgasm. This moment, however, hinged on an even more profound level of gratitude. Hal had helped me to actualise my inner animal. He had been my obsession, and had allowed me to step into a new gender role for both our sakes. For each of us, our enjoyment hinged on the other's satisfaction and that was a kind of symbiosis with which I had not been familiar until that moment.

I felt, for the first time in my life...that I had met my match. That Hal and I were able to share this kind of interaction was more than just a bonus.

"Don't tell Aunt Myrtle," I teased.

Chapter Fifteen

We went on to fuck each other in all kinds of unimaginable ways. He took my cock regularly and I came easily from penetrating him. I learned how to position my harness even better as time went on, and we became so well versed in our own special language that we forgot all about the codes of what was considered normal sex. He never penetrated me and I didn't want him to. Whenever the desire for sex came upon us, we each assumed these selves that we could be when we were together.

We were both quite different than we had been in any other context. I believe that is a sign of true intimacy. It isn't trusting your partner to keep secrets for you, or even to please you or let you please yourself. It's being able to be unencumbered around that person, and free to express things that have hitherto seemed impossible. In our case, these things were not verbal, but intensely corporeal.

Once in a while, a deep need for an old-fashioned fuck would set in and I'd make an appointment with Simon. Somewhat predictably, the situation between us had become complicated. His love for me was wrapped up in expectations of allegiance. I did not understand how he had the audacity to even consider monogamy with me, but he told me in no uncertain terms that he would always be faithful to me.

I insisted that he sleep around. I argued that I was but one flavour, and that he was a young man, and it was more than natural that he should have urges that I could not fulfil. He disappointed me by investing too much attention in our relationship. His stakes were high. Too high. I had no real interest in the boy. He was a brilliant distraction, beautifully crafted, much like the garments he designed.

Inevitably, his time came and he had to leave Virginia. It wasn't without regret on my part. I had enjoyed being in his studio whenever I grew bored of Strawberry Hill. He offered the kind of interactions that few men could. He gave me the intellectual satisfaction of a good sparring partner, coupled with the kind of attention that Hal didn't give me. Hal loved me, I was sure. But Hal and I both shared a streak of belligerence. Neither of us could bow down in the way Simon could. That was why Hal was my partner and why Simon eventually became obsolete.

His submission, the very reason I was initially attracted to him, became too much for me to handle, and so I stopped. I simply stopped. I stopped visiting him. I stopped making appointments and, most importantly, I stopped thinking about him in his absence. He took a job with a prestigious designer in New York City. I was happy for him, as was Hal.

When he left, Simon told me he would keep in touch, but I didn't believe him and I was proved right. Some things are just meant to be temporary, and I still believe that he benefitted from my tutelage just as I benefitted from his meekness.

I had plenty of others to choose from at Strawberry Hill but, after Simon left, I mostly took to exploring Hal. I also became enamoured with a different kind of luxury — reading. I studied as much as I could. Hal supported me fully. His benefactor conferred property rights on him. The authorities granted him his status and we lived a comfortable, quiet life of mutual understanding. It was the first time in my life that I had had access to the kind of time and money that Hal provided, and it was strange at first. I didn't know how to pass the days. I stayed fit by running because there was no need to tend to the garden. We had professionals for that. There was no need to cook or clean, as we had full-time employees to do that, too.

Luckily for me, I'd always had a passion for books. I started in Hal's library, which he had inherited from his benefactor, who was a scholar of the highest status. I didn't know where to begin, which is the beauty of innocence, and so I just began. After several years, I started to make sense of the order in which it happened. Romantics, Modernists, then Greeks. Finally, contemporary. It just happened that way. It was accidental. But it did follow a symbolic path of my life, allowing me to relive feelings and expressions of my past. I learned to reinterpret my life. I learned to find pleasure in sounds and sights and I learned to open my mind even further than I had ever imagined.

One day, a letter arrived from Kelly. My heart pounded when I saw her name. The return address was a small town in Oregon, which shocked me. Instantly, my feelings for her came rushing back. The intensity of those early days, how different I had been then, how utterly foreign it felt to hear from her.

I opened the envelope and read the purple-penned note. One of her biggest regrets, she wrote, was the way she'd turned me down. It had haunted her, the way it haunts every lesbian who finally makes sense of her whole existence when she meets that one person—that first true love who invites her into the Sapphic embrace. Her explanation made perfect sense and ended with a sincere invitation for me to visit her and Laurel at their goat farm.

I packed a suitcase and booked a flight and, when Hal came home that afternoon, I kissed him on the cheek and said, "I'm going to Oregon."

"What's in Oregon?"

"A girl. Kelly."

"Oooh." He gave me a flirtatious grin.

"It's not like that," I said.

"She's straight?" He affected a mope.

"Partnered," I said.

"So are you." He winked.

"You dirty dog, Hal. She's just come out to me and wants me to meet her lover."

"That sounds like fun to me," he said. We kissed. I flung my arms around him and held him tightly. Everything about Hal was perfect to me.

* * * *

I pulled up to the address less than twenty-four hours after I'd got Kelly's letter. There were butterflies in my tummy and I could scarcely believe where I was. So rugged and woodsy was this place that it had been nearly impossible to convince a taxi driver to take me. I'd had to promise to give him a massive tip, which was my pleasure. I loved being able to offer more money for services. He pulled up at the end of a driveway that was practically a road — that was how long it was. I opened the door and looked up at the house, a rustic log home, completely different from what I'd imagined. I didn't know what I had expected, but it hadn't been this.

"Julie?" I heard Kelly's voice. "Is that you?"

She came running and threw her arms around me. Her hair smelt divine, her figure pressed up against me and we were as we had been before. She was a true friend.

"Let me get a good look at you," she pulled back, beaming her beautiful smile at me. She looked so alive, so vibrant.

"Oh, Kelly. I have missed you. I was so glad you wrote."

"I thought about it long and hard. I wondered if you'd even want to hear from me."

"Of course I did."

She pulled my suitcase out of the trunk. I handed a wad of cash to the driver and, before I knew it, we were on her back porch, soaking up the last rays of the day's sun. A little after dark, Laurel came home, joined us on the patio and kissed the top of Kelly's head before she extended her hand to me.

"Welcome," she said. "Kelly's told me so much about you."

"Thanks for having me," I said.

With that, Laurel announced that she'd crack open a special bottle of chardonnay from her friend's vineyard, one she had been saving for a special occasion. Her eyes were warm and inviting and I could tell that Kelly had found in her the kind of lasting love I'd found with Hal. This observation was a sheer delight. As the wine flowed, so did the conversation. I learned that Laurel and Kelly had also met in San Francisco, that Laurel had also fallen madly and hopelessly in love with Kelly. The difference, it seemed, was that Laurel had known exactly how to communicate her feelings. She'd known what she wanted. It might have helped that they'd met at a coffee shop, not at Kelly's workplace.

"I was finally ready to face my feelings," Kelly said. Laurel, who was sitting right beside her, hanging on her every word, put her hand on Kelly's back and rubbed it. They locked eyes. "I was finally ready to admit something I'd always known but couldn't accept. And then, almost overnight, my life filled with joy and peace and I knew exactly what I wanted to do, so I cashed in my tokens."

"And I quit my horrible office job," Laurel added, making it clear that they'd co-told this story many times before.

Kelly continued, "And we bought this place and now we make cheese. We keep bees, too. I have to take you on a walking tour of the property. There's a lake down there, too." She pointed towards what appeared to be a dense forest.

"Amazing," I said. "To finding happiness." We clinked glasses. It was a toast I'd wanted to give for a long time.

As the night continued, I felt as though I was in the company of two kindred spirits. I let my guard down completely and it felt great.

"I think I hated men when I was younger," I confessed. "I resented their power and thought I had to make it in a man's world."

"You did," Kelly said. "Make it, I mean."

"I love you so much, Kelly. You understand me in ways no one else ever will."

"I could say the same," she said.

Laurel got up and went into the house. She re-emerged with a lantern, a basket of towels and three pairs of flip-flops and announced that it was time for me to see the lake.

After a sultry evening of lake swimming, Kelly said she was sincerely looking forward to meeting Hal.

I embraced her lovingly and said, "That's the nicest thing you could ever tell me."

"Do you think he'll like me?" she wanted to know.

"I can't imagine anyone not liking you, Kelly. Really."

* * * *

A week later, Laurel and Kelly and I pulled into the driveway at Strawberry Hill on a glorious sunny afternoon. Unsurprisingly, Hal was phenomenal. He came out and greeted us by kissing me and offering a friendly hug to Kelly and Laurel.

"I've arranged for mint juleps in the gazebo," he said.

"I haven't had one of those in ages," Kelly said, letting herself expose the accent she so often covered up.

"Julie told me you're from Alabama," Hal said.

"I am. Good to be back in the South."

"Isn't it, though?" Hal said. "We're having barbecue later."

It was lovely being back. Strawberry Hill was home. So was Hal. He was more than a husband—he was a true partner in my life, letting me explore as I wished and supporting me throughout.

We sat in the gazebo, chatting and laughing as the sun set over the lush green horizon. In the warm dusk hues, I was surrounded by love. I don't think it is possible to feel more appreciation than I did that late summer evening.

About the Author

Destiny Moon has lived in Europe, Africa and North America.

She always dreamt of becoming the kind of writer people would read with a flash light under the covers or covertly on the bus.

Destiny Moon loves to hear from readers. You can find her contact information, website details and author profile page at http://www.total-e-bound.com.

Total-E-Bound Publishing

www.total-e-bound.com

Take a look at our exciting range of literagasmic™
erotic romance titles and discover pure quality
at Total-E-Bound.